Houdini

T. J. Banks

PublishingWorks
Exeter, NH

Copyright © T. J. Banks 2008. All rights reserved.
Illustrations © Linda Zak 2008.

PublishingWorks, Inc.
151 Epping Rd.
Exeter, NH 03833
603-778-9883

For Sales and Orders:
1-800-738-6603 or 603-772-7200
www.publishingworks.com

Designed by Kat Mack
Cover Image by Caron Wiedrick ~ http://artsofeden.com

LCCN: 2007934598
ISBN: 1-933002-57-3
ISBN–13: 978-1-933002-57-6

Houdini

For Marissa and the cats in her life—especially Cricket, Topaz, and our grand old man, Dervish, who, after 19 years of big-pawed, big-hearted companionship, traveled to a world beyond our seeing. We miss you, Derv—nobody did friendship better.

ACKNOWLEDGMENTS

Like Beatrix Potter's Tailor of Gloucester, I had a lot of behind-the-scenes help. Among that help were two of the best editors I've ever worked with, Nancy and Bob Hungerford, who were the first to read parts of *Houdini* and who showed their faith in it—and in me—by running an excerpt from it in their award-winning publication, *Just Cats!* That excerpt went on to win a Certificate of Excellence from the Cat Writers' Association back in 1994. Kim Cady is another fine editor who has showed her support by publishing several excerpts on her website, cleverkitty.org. Then there were the good souls who gave their support in one way or another: the late Cleveland Amory of The Fund for Animals, Inc., who wrote of my feline hero, "What a sweet, loyal soul. And what a brave one, to boot"; Rita Reynolds, editor of *la Joie: The Journal That Honors All Beings* ; Cynthia Daffion; Maria L. Hampton; Thomas D. Morganti, DVM; and Amy D. Shojai of the Cat Writers' Association.

As always, I am grateful to my publisher, Jeremy Townsend, for many things, especially for her supportiveness and her sense of humor. Thanks to Linda Mailly Zak for her talented and heart-felt illustrations and to Caron Wiedrick and Shai for the wonderful cover photo that captures the soul of *Houdini*.

Then there are two other faithful friends and supporters who must be listed: my late mother-in-law, Barbara S. Spooner—a writer in her own right and "a good in-between-times person, Tam," as she once assured me—and my late grandmother-in-law, Dorothy F. Skinner, the inimitable "Fitz." But my deepest appreciation goes to the person whose belief in me never wavered, even when my own did: my late husband, Tim Spooner, who dragged me, as he put it, "kicking and screaming into the computer age," and who remarked after helping me set *Houdini* into proper computerese, "I found myself wanting to read the next page. That says something." It did indeed, for he wasn't a person who gave praise lightly or who damned with faint praise (actually, he made a point of skipping the faint-praise part entirely). Perhaps, in the end, his remains for me the greatest tribute that *Houdini* ever received. It was certainly the hardest won.

1

The Flame point Siamese kitten opened his blue eyes and yawned. His were sapphire-blue eyes, not that pale almost milky-blue that turns to green, gold, or copper within a few weeks. He stretched a long absurdly big reddish-gold front paw (he would, in time, grow into those paws) out of the carton he'd curled up in the night before, when the humans had been bustling around with bigger boxes, brushing him aside when he'd rubbed up against them, hungry for pats. But surely this morning they'd have time for him. And food. They'd forgotten to feed him last night: his stomach was so empty, it hurt him. Usually, the girls just gave him scraps and milk, whatever they happened to have on hand. But sometimes there was tuna fish. And once, sardines. The kitten gave his left front paw a lick at the memory and hopped out of the box.

The on-campus apartment had a strange, cold silence about it. Most of the blinds ... the ones that weren't broken, just hanging, barely in place with their slats half off, that is . . . were drawn, making the room a dark, unfriendly place to a small animal who wanted food and cuddling. This darkness wasn't natural, and it frightened the kitten, who, at two pounds, could neatly fit into an adult human hand.

He took a few timid steps forward and let loose a hoarse, sad "Wah-ah!" No high-pitched voices calling back in answer, no funny high heels clicking away on the worn, cheap kitchen linoleum. Kerflummoxed, the kitten sat down on his satiny-soft haunches and pondered the situation. He glanced around but saw nothing except a black beetle, the kind he sometimes liked to play with. He flipped it over onto its back and moved in for the crunch, then remembered how he'd bitten into a similar bug the week before and how long it had taken him to shake the sour taste from his mouth. So he let this one right itself and scurry off behind the counter.

He sniffed the air, but there were none of those flowery scents that he'd come to associate with the girls' grooming. No cooking smells coming out of the tiny box of a kitchen either. The silence was as thick as the big pink plaid afghan that one of the girls used to let him sleep on. No, he told himself, they were definitely gone, taking with them all their peculiar human gear, all the traces of their life here. Except for him.

Not that they hadn't left him before. Often, they'd disappeared for hours, coming in late at night and shooing him off whichever bed he'd been sleeping on. But this felt different. His growing cat-sense told him they weren't coming back this time.

He put his whole heart into wailing then. "Wahwuh-wah!" the kitten cried out into the empty room, his Siamese voice ricocheting off the peeling poster-less plaster walls. He kept it up until his voice finally gave out. Then he curled himself into a miserable little white ball and, wrapping his reddish-gold tail around his paws, lost himself in sleep.

When the kitten awoke hours later, the hunger was almost unbearable. He caught a couple of beetles and managed to worry them down despite their awful taste; they didn't scare the hunger away completely, but they kept it at bay a bit.

He headed into the tiny bathroom, searching for his litter box; but that, too, was gone. Frantically, he scratched at the linoleum, then, thinking better of it, the kitten jumped up onto the sink and used the badly cracked basin. He scuffed at the porcelain in a desperate reach for his litter-box manners, then hopped back down onto the floor.

He wandered into the taller girl's bedroom, one of his favorite napping places because of the way the afternoon sun came filtering in through the blinds that she generally left open. Today, however, the blinds were pulled tightly shut. This room was, he realized, empty, too, except for the dust-mice who lived under the bed.

He poked his nose into the open closet. Another kitten—ivory-white with a reddish-gold Siamese mask, ears, leggings, and tail, just like his—peered at him from around the doorway. The kitten hissed and drew back. Then he stretched a curious paw out toward the intruder, who did likewise. The little Siamese cocked his head to one side; puzzled, he moved closer and put his paw up to the other's face. But instead of fur and whisker, he touched something hard and cold and flat. Something that seemed to be fastened on the inside of the door. Several times, the kitten leaped up at the glassy surface that separated him from this other kitten so like himself: each time, the other mimicked his sparring moves, its blue eyes just as wide and curious as his own. Finally, he realized that there was no way that the kitten-in-the-glass could get out, and he turned away, lonelier than ever.

He made his way into the shorter girl's room and hopped up onto one of the wide windowsills. In her hurry to get packed and out of there, she'd forgotten to close this particular window. He couldn't escape into the Great Unknown Outside—there was a screen—but he could at least get some fresh air. "Wah-wuh-wah!" the kitten cried, hooking his tiny, sharp claws into the mesh. "Wah-wuh-wah!" What humans he did see on the sidewalk below just kept on moving, passing by without even a half-glance upwards. He might as well have been the kitten-in-the-glass. He laid down on the sill and rested his head on his paws, his eyes a thoughtful, worried, slightly-crossed blue.

The sun on his back was as warm as his mother's tongue had been, but it raised his spirits about as much as the bugs had curbed his appetite. He glanced out the window again: there were still a few humans strolling about on the other side of the street, but they seemed very far away to him. Then he heard the heels. Short chunky ones clopping along at an easy, rhythmic pace on the sidewalk closest to his window. He sat up and tilted his head to the side, listening. Pretty soon, a short messy-haired man in a nondescript old jacket came ambling into view. Leaping up, the kitten hooked his front claws back into the screen and began wailing out all the hunger and loneliness he'd been feeling.

The stranger halted and glanced quickly around him. As soon as he caught sight of the kitten hanging off the screen, he hurried over. He murmured something from his side of the window. The kitten heard the kindness in his voice and let go of his grip on the screen, one paw at a time. He began kneading the windowsill with its grungy, peeling paint—he was so happy. "Mer-row," he told this new friend, blinking up at him.

The man touched the kitten's face through the wire mesh. "Be right back, little fella," he said and disappeared quickly back around the corner. . . . The minutes crept by, more slowly than a kitten just learning to walk. Finally, there was a rattling at the door, which made the little Siamese's sailboat ears perk up. The man came in with a woman whose voice and movements were familiar to him. A woman with warm brown skin, kind dark eyes, and a lilting voice. She came to clean the apartment periodically and always petted and talked to him. Sometimes she let him chase her broom or feather duster.

"Can you believe those jerks?" the young man, David, was saying angrily to Julia, the cleaning woman. He glanced around the stripped-down room. "Leaving an animal in this place without food and water—acting like it's some kind of toy!"

Julia pocketed her keys and sighed. "These kids, they do it all the time," she said. "I don't understand it either." She went over to the window and gently scooped the kitten up in her arms. He snuggled up against her breasts and, in a series of plaintive almost bleating "mer-rows," told her about How Lonely and Frightened He'd Been. "He's so pretty. And so friendly. I never knew a cat to talk so much, just like a person." She smiled down at the kitten, then looked up at the young grad student, her brown eyes questioning.

He walked over to where she was standing and scritched the kitten under the chin. "Sure is cute." The kitten blinked at him again and began purring at his rescuers. "I can't take him, not with my dog. But my buddy, Jim, has family staying over with him for his wedding, and the kid—well, she's sick and missing her own cat back home. . . ." He shrugged. "It's worth a shot, I guess." He eased the kitten out of the woman's arms. "Thanks for letting me in, Julia—I'll take over from here." He zipped the burbling little Siamese up into his jacket. "How many does this make that we've rescued this semester?"

"Three or four," she answered, smiling sadly.

The kitten made himself comfortable inside the jacket, doing push-me-pull-you's with his snippet-claws in and out of the young man's rumpled blue cotton shirt. The man, David, held him securely, one hand braced under the jacketed bottom to keep the long-ish hind legs from dangling. The kitten forgot about the girls leaving him like that, forgot about the empty rooms and the emptier food dish, and forgot about the lonely kitten-in-the-mirror. He poked his head a little further out of the jacket and sniffed the early May air, his long whiskers aquiver with the scents of birds and blossoms and freshly mowed grass. Then the bigness of it got to be too much for him, and he burrowed his face against David's old shirt. "It's OK, buddy," the young man laughed softly. "Got you covered."

They came to a white two-family house at the end of a shady side street. David rapped on the door; the kitten played with the dog tags around his protector's neck while they waited. After a few seconds, they heard footsteps, and another, taller man opened the door. The Siamese kept up with his dog-tag game (OK, so they weren't catnip mice—he'd had one once, and it had been a kitten's dream come true—but they made Great Noise) while they talked. Then, his ears perking up at the slightly higher, questioning note in David's voice, he glanced up at this new stranger, a metal tag dangling from his baby fangs.

Jimmy shook his head and laughed. "OK, OK," he said, raising his hands in mock surrender. "Bring the crazy cat in before he strangles you." They headed down the hallway with all its colorful artistic clutter and stopped at a half-opened door to the right. This room was crammed with unframed paintings and collages and an old Coke machine that had been picked up at a flea market somewhere. There was an old-fashioned brass bed over by the window and a fold-away cot jammed up against the opposite wall. In the latter was the little girl that David had been telling Julia about, sitting up, her eyes widening as she caught sight of the little cat face peering out over the zipper of his jacket.

Going over to her now, the short man undid his jacket and placed the kitten alongside her on the faded coverlet. "Found him all alone in one of those campus apartments," he growled. "Stupid, rotten people moved out and left him there."

The girl, Jill, reached out a small hand toward the kitten and smoothed his satiny fur. "Thank you," she said shyly, the dullness fading from her dark eyes.

David pulled out a crooked grin for her. "No problem, kid." He scratched his head and turned to his friend. "Say, Jim, I gotta be getting back to the library and finishing up some work I left in my carrel. I'll see you before the big family dinner tomorrow night?"

"Yeah, sure. You think you could pick up some art books for me while you're there?" Jimmy asked, reaching into his paint-spattered shirt pocket. "I got the names on a piece of paper here." He frowned as his hand came up empty. "No, I guess it's somewhere in that big pile of papers out on the table in the other room." He glanced his niece's way. "Get some rest, George," he said, using his pet name for her. "We'll rig up a place for your cat friend later."

She barely noticed them leaving the room, her eyes were so taken up with the kitten. Never had she seen a Siamese with his colors before. And he wanted to be loved so badly—she could tell by his eyes and the way he kept kneading the bedclothes—she just couldn't imagine anyone abandoning him like David said those people had. Jill reached out her hand to him again, still amazed at finding this exotic little purebred hers (she was sure that he was one—he looked just like a Flame point Siamese she'd seen in a magazine). He butted his head against the hand she offered him, purring like he had a world of purring to catch up on.

Which, in a sense, he did. He climbed up onto her chest and rubbed his face against hers, making her his. She giggled at the ticklish feel of his whiskers, and he did it again. Then he curled up on her shoulder, pressing his long muzzle against the side of her throat. He gave his red-gold paws a good stretch and squunked happily, forgetting his hunger—well, for the moment, anyway—in his joy at finding a human who needed him as much as he needed her.

Later that day, when Jill was feeling better, Jimmy kept his promise and helped her "rig up" a sleeping place for the kitten. They lined a big cardboard carton with newspapers; then, seeing that the flaps would have to be folded shut at night or any time they went out to keep him from getting into trouble, they poked a slew of holes in the sides with some old drawing pencils. Then, while her uncle was outside, fixing up a makeshift litter box, the girl set up his food and water dishes—two chipped and cracked Blue Willow-ware dishes, flea-market finds that Jimmy had told her she could have from the kitchen—alongside the carton.

"C'mon, kitty," Jill called softly. His true name still hadn't come to her. "Come see your new apartment."

The kitten, his little Siamese heart already fixed on her, already attune to the rhythms of her voice and her movements, trotted on over. He checked out the food dish first, of course; but since he'd already wolfed down all those slices of deli meat out in the kitchen earlier, he didn't spend too much time over it. Then he gave the box itself a good once-over, rubbing his chin against the flaps and corners, marking it for his own. He hopped in and nuzzled the faded turquoise T-shirt that Jill had put in there for him to sleep on. It smelled pleasantly of his new girl, and he blinked up at her approvingly, then did a few push-me-pull-you's on the soft fabric to get it just right for a little after-lunch snooze. But just before he put his head down for the count, he shot one more glance up at Jill to make sure that she hadn't gone away on him like his other humans had.

Jill studied the tiny rounded masked face with the absurdly long nose affectionately. She had seen Siamese cats before—some friends of her parents' had a crotchety old one who knocked the jewelry off the woman's bureau and stashed it under the rug whenever they went out—but, except for the cat in the magazine picture, never one all white-and-gold like this, the soft tones making his blue eyes stand out all the more and giving him an incredibly angelic look.

He looks like Kimba, Jill thought suddenly, calling to mind the white lion cub in the cartoon she'd watched back in first grade. She'd loved that orphaned cub so much, she'd wanted a white lion cub of her very own until one of her older brothers, Rob, had explained to her how unfair it would be to take any animal out of the wild like that. . . .

"Kimba," she said softly, stroking the drowsy kitten's sailboat ears. But even as she said it, Jill knew it wasn't the right name. Almost, but not quite. She glanced down and saw that he'd fallen asleep, one paw over his eyes. Unable to resist, she slipped her hand gently under his long tail and tucked it under the paw. The kitten never budged. Wonder what he'll think happened when he wakes up? she thought, grinning. She folded the box's flaps shut and tiptoed away.

The kitten awoke hours later. There was a strange ticklish feeling around his eyes that startled, even worried him a bit. He clawed at the mysterious creature who'd taken the light away with it, only to find out that the beast in question was his own tail. It was a long tail, and he found considerable satisfaction in beating it up. Victorious, he sat up, scrubbed his face, and polished off his paws. It was dark in the box... though not half so dark as before... and a loneliness, as large and thick as the night itself, took hold of him as he began to fret about where his girl had gone off to without him.

He poked and poked at the top of the box, finally forcing his paw through the small opening where the flaps came together and the moonlight crept in. The cardboard was old, and those folds had gotten more than a little bent during the tucking-in process. It wasn't that difficult for a small kitten to push and prod at them until he was able to create a large enough space for him to wriggle out of. The carton sat right alongside Jill's cot. He hopped up onto the bed and trotted over to the pillow. The honeysuckle-shampoo scent of her thick, curly hair lingered there, warm and comforting. He pushed his way under the pillow until he'd made a little cave for himself, then curled up and waited.

Finally, he heard her quick, light footsteps tapping along down the hallway and into the room. When she didn't come over to him right away, he let loose one of those funny "mer-rows" of his that always made him sound more like an indignant sheep than a kitten.

Jill hurried over to the cot and peered under the humped-up pillow. The kitten peered back at her, his eyes large, lonely, and very crossed. Unable to get back into the carton, where his litter box was situated, he wet the section of sheet underneath the pillow. Jill wrinkled her nose slightly, then made up her mind that she wouldn't let the adults know about it; they'd only raise a ruckus about it, and, besides, it wasn't as if the poor little guy could've helped it. She'd clean up the bed in the morning herself. She pulled the kitten out of his pillow-lair; then, grabbing the T-shirt out of the box, she covered up the damp spot with it. That done, she crawled into bed, and the kitten snuggled up against her cheek. He was so happy to have her back with him, he washed the inside of the ear closest to him and all of her eyelashes, trilling happily away at her the entire time. She wasn't Going Away again, was she? he demanded, nipping her earlobe lovingly. Ignoring her yelp, he stretched a front paw out on either shoulder and watched her out of blissful half-shut eyes before falling off to sleep again.

The next night, he was sitting on top of the pillow when she came in. And purring so hard, she thought his little body would burst.

II

One morning, a few days later, the kitten found himself being placed in a smaller box. The inside was lined with newspaper; underneath that was a layer of tin foil (the foil would keep the box from leaking on the plane—or so Jill hoped). The girl had also tucked in a catnip mouse that she'd picked up from the five-and-ten down the street, figuring that it would give him something to snuggle up against during the long flight home.

The kitten butted his head anxiously against her hand as she gave him one last pat before tucking the flaps in. He tried to peer through the pencil-holes she'd poked into the top and the sides, but he couldn't make out much, only flashes of skin and eye. And he couldn't be too sure about that eye either. He lay down, his body aquiver, and waited to see what would happen next.

After what seemed a long time to his kitten-brain, he felt the box being lifted up into the air and carried away. Then there were the sounds and smells: doors opening and closing, a whiff of fresh morning air and honeysuckle, the gabble of human voices, and a loud growling noise, which he thought must come from some large animal. He flattened his ears and tried to make himself very small, just in case it could see him through the holes. The Beast must've grabbed the box and started to run with it, for suddenly he was moving so fast, his empty stomach flip-flopped. He cried out for his girl. Then he heard her voice murmuring gently to him from somewhere just outside his box, and he relaxed slightly, knowing that she was nearby. That she wouldn't let the Beast eat him. Still trembling, he wrapped his long tail around his paws and held himself in check. Maybe, if he was lucky—very, very lucky—the Beast wouldn't smell his fear.

The Creature finally stopped moving, worn out with all its running, no doubt. There were more doors slamming, more voices talking over each other in that loud, jarring way that humans had, and more feet scrabbling over a hard surface of some sort. Somebody must've taken the box away from That Creature—somebody with strong arms and a sweaty, outdoorsy smell. Probably his girl's father, who liked to tickle the kitten's belly and paw-wrestle with him. But Jill herself was somewhere close by, his senses told him. He had to hold on to that. It was, he told himself, looking down his long nose—for he was a reflective kitten—a Matter of Faith.

Jill's father, Mr. Leonard, glanced about a little too casually as they boarded the plane. Their seats were in front. He got in first, and, with a quick nod to his wife, who was sitting across the aisle from them, he stowed the cardboard carton underneath his seat. Jill scooted in after her father, wondering if that pretty blonde stewardess had noticed the quivering box and if her parents really had been right about not feeding the little guy before the long trip. She sighed and pulled a well-creased copy of Mary Calhoun's *The House of Thirty Cats* out of her tote bag.

Peering out of one of the bigger holes, the kitten could just about make out part of his girl's navy-blue sneaker resting alongside the box. He tried to poke his paw out of the hole and make a grab for her lace. Just a little tug to remind her that He was There. But he couldn't force his paw through, no matter how hard he clawed and prodded.

A newer—and stranger—sound came at him now, a high-pitched whooshing one that hurt his ears. The air itself felt different, too—closer, less breathable—though he couldn't quite put his paw on why it should be.

"Wah-wuh-wah!" he wailed. He thought he heard Jill's soft voice answering him back, but he couldn't have sworn to it. So he kept crying out for her, wondering why she didn't come and let him out of this box, which was so much less roomy and comfortable than the one he'd had in the spare room.

Jill, meanwhile, kept darting agonized glances at the box at her dad's feet. She swallowed hard. "Can't I take him out and hold him, Dad?" she blurted at last.

"No," Mr. Leonard said, his teeth clenched. "You wanna get us thrown off the damn plane?" And he muttered something else under his breath.

She bit back a sigh and tried to focus on her book. Which, normally, wouldn't have been too hard—it was, after all, one of her favorites. But her eyes kept returning guiltily to that small miaowing box.

The shrill cries eventually gave way to soft baby kittenish whimpering. Just when the Flame point had practically cried himself out, the box opened up, and a beautiful lady in a dark-blue uniform and cap was lifting him up and cooing over him. She carried him, all soiled and smelly as he was, over to where two other women in similar uniforms sat. They all took turns patting and fussing over him, telling him in their mourning-dove voices how pretty he was. Purring, he closed his eyes and did push-paws on the first stewardess' knee.

She laughed as she unhooked his claws from her nylons. "You'll have to take him into the men's room and clean him up when we get to Chicago," she told Mr. Leonard.

He nodded and put on his best smile for her, trying (Jill thought) to look as though he hadn't been tempted to open his window and send the little guy parachuting down to earth, minus the parachute. Not that he really would've done it, even if he could've—her father was as kind as he was quick-tempered—but it was funny to see him swallow his anger so charmingly.

The stewardess handed the kitten back to Mr. Leonard, who promptly popped him back into the box. The kitten snuggled back down among the fresh newspapers that the man had put in there while he was gone. He was dirty and hungry, but at least easy in his mind that His New Humans Hadn't Forgotten Him, like the first ones had.

Pretty soon, there was a gradual downward motion that came to an abrupt halt. Then someone (the girl's father again, he thought) picked up the box and began walking away with it. The kitten tensed up at the loud, harsh noises that were bombarding him through the holes: he flattened his ears like an angry little bobcat and dug his claws into the newspapers as another human (at least, he hoped it was another human, given how strange and nightmarish his little world had become) jostled against the box. But in a moment or two, he felt the carton being set down again; then, suddenly, it was open, and the girl was lifting him up. "Nyeh-nyeh-nawh," he told her, then launched into a series of plaintive yowls about The Beast and The Terrible, Dark Place. Not that he held her responsible, he assured her (though he gave her a slightly reproachful look), but he really thought she should know about The Ordeal He Had Gone Through and What a Brave Kitten He'd Been.

Jill's dad strolled over and waited for her to hand the kitten over so that he could wrap him up in what was left of the newspaper and cart him off to the washroom. There, the little guy squawked unmercifully in his most Siamese of voices about the funny-smelling soap, the cold water, and the rough brown paper towels. Afterwards, however, when the man carried him back to the waiting area (this time, tucked inside the blue sports jacket, his whiskered flame-tinged face poking out over the top button), the kitten preened himself a bit and checked out the herds of people roaming about the huge drafty place with wide-eyed interest.

But he couldn't check them out for long. No, he had to go back into That Box again. He miaowed a nails-on-chalkboard protest, which didn't sway Mr. Leonard in the least. "In you go," the latter said, pushing an angry paw gently back into the carton and closing its flaps. "You're banished." The kitten settled back down, huffily, nattering to himself as only an affronted Siamese can. Still, Jill had cleaned out his quarters as much as possible and re-lined them with a newspaper somebody had left lying on the seat next to hers at the airport. He could barely feel the scratchy, crinkly tin foil underneath. He dozed off in spite of himself, worn out from his crying and his bath.

Before he knew it, he was being lifted out of the hated carton again. He blinked sleepily at the girl and put a paw up to her face. She propped him up parrot-style on her shoulder. He purred (now this was really more like it, he decided) and fell to studying the inside of her ear. Definitely overdue for a wash, he decided. Once he'd taken care of that order of business, he started studying this latest change of scenery, trying to get his bearings. They were riding in yet another Rumble-Beast, but after the Terrible Whooshing Thing (which must've been a bird, he decided), it didn't scare him all that much. Actually, the rumbling sounded to him a lot like a loud, ragged purring, as if this particular

Beast had forgotten how to purr and was learning how to do it all over again. A tall young man with dark hair and a mustache sat in the front with the girl's parents; it looked to the kitten as though he was guiding the Beast along. Ah. A Tamed Beast. The kitten blinked his eyes approvingly. Nothing to worry about. His Journey, he figured, would be an uneventful one from now on.

A skinny boy with curly, dark hair and eyes like the girl's—another brother, Scott—was hanging out in the back seat with them. Jill lifted the Siamese off her shoulder so that Scott could get a better look at him. She told him about the kitten's Great Escape from the box that first night in Oklahoma. Scott laughed. "You'll have to call him 'Houdini' then," he told her, grinning.

She grinned back at her brother. Houdini. Of course. Why hadn't she thought of that? she asked herself. It was so simple, and it fit him just like his satiny white fur with its reddish-gold points. No Kimba or Puff for a spunky kitten like this, she thought, quickly moving her hand as he got too playful and began giving her hand little nips. And it would suit him just as well when he grew into those long paws and huge ears of his some day....

III

Houdini slept on Jill's bed that first night. The next morning, however, she set up a place for him on the large enclosed porch off the kitchen. It was, she knew, a temporary arrangement: she'd have to take him outside for short periods of time until he and the other cats-in-residence had gotten used to each other. Then he'd have to go live with them outside in the tool shed. No matter how much Jill pled or pouted, Mr. Leonard wouldn't budge on this one point. He loved animals—almost as much as his daughter did—but he'd been raised on a farm, and he just didn't see why anybody would want to keep cats in the house. Oh, they could come in for their "visits" or if they were sick or hurt—he didn't have a problem with that, and when they were ill, he doctored them with a gentleness that belied his sometimes rough manner—but they were animals, all the same, and they belonged outdoors at night or when Jill was at school. And she had to go along with it, much as she wished she didn't have to. Over the years, many of the kittens and more than a few of the cats had gotten hit by cars or simply disappeared, picked off by either disease or the coyotes that Jill and her brothers had sometimes spotted in the field out in back.

Houdini didn't mind the porch—although, of course, he much preferred Jill's bed with its soft blankets and squishy pillows with their great kitten-cave potential. But the porch had its good points, too. There were lots of wooden milk crates and cardboard boxes stacked all along the barn-board walls that he could scrabble or leap (although his jumps weren't always very successful when it came to the higher stacks) on top of or hide behind, ready to pounce on some unwary human foot. The room also had jalousie windows on three sides that he could peer out of.

And there was plenty for him to peer out at, too. Maple trees with good thick climbable trunks and lilacs already past their bloom but leafy enough to make for cool, dark hiding places. Blue jays and mocking-birds setting the air aquiver with their cries and chipmunks that set his tail twitching furiously. Some older cats and a couple of kittens who were just about his size. He clawed at the screens and "yaowed" out at them. The kittens, as curious about him as he'd been about the kitten-in-the-glass, glanced up and mewed back. But the adults simply acted as if he wasn't there.

A few mornings after his arrival, Jill took Houdini out into the yard for the first time. He stepped gingerly through the grass, his sapphire eyes wide and shimmering. The cats he'd been tracking from the porch windows began to materialize out of nowhere, crouching under the maple and pine trees and watching him out of their large, unblinking green or amber eyes. Houdini rolled over and thrust his soft white underbelly upwards, eager to show them that he meant no harm. But they just kept staring at him, their tails swishing judgmentally back and forth.

One long-haired brown tiger kitten with a white ruff and paws came as close as the edge of the garden. Another kitten, all plushy gray, white, and orange fur with an absurd little patchwork mask to match, joined her. They studied him thoughtfully for a bit; then the long-haired kitten began to pick her way daintily toward him. Intrigued,

Houdini got up on his feet and trotted over to meet her. The garden was thick with velvety-leaved Persian and lemon catnip, white-blossomed lemon balm, and balloon flowers bursting into wide-petaled blue and white flowers. There were snapdragons, too—butterflies of coral, crimson, yellow, and white nestling against the rich, dark earth—white-starred thyme, and tall swaying-in-the-wind purply harebells and hostas. A pair of goldfinches fluttered about the catnip, practically seesawing on the tough woody stalks. They flew off as Houdini neared them; but he barely noted them. So intent he was on the fluffy kitten.

She sat down within a paw's-length of him and opened her mouth in a tiny feminine hiss. Houdini raised his right paw as if to strike her, but it was really all for show. After a few more formalities of this type, the girl kitten, Juliet, turned playful. They nibbled companionably at the catnip together, then began rolling on the ground, waving their paws at each other in mock battle-style.

The calico kit, Dimity, was just joining them when a lean, golden-red tabby with a long, snaky tail bounded into the garden. Juliet and Dimity fled under the hedge near the old green tool shed. Ears flat against his bullet-shaped head and tail puffed out like a woolly-bear caterpillar, the tomcat lunged at Houdini, thwapping him hard on the ears.

With a shriek, Houdini raced over to where Jill sat on the back-porch stoop and leapt onto her lap. He scrambled up onto her shoulder, mer-rowing loudly and piteously about This New Danger and demanding that she Do Something about It. She laughed a little and smoothed his fur until his tail got less bottle-brushy and settled back into place.

Relaxing his grip on her, Houdini gave his own shoulder a few licks and glanced about him nervously. Juliet and Dimity had seemingly vanished, although he thought he caught a glimpse of the calico's large pale-green eyes peering out of the shadowy little cat-door in the front of the shed. In fact, the yard was suddenly and mysteriously empty of cats, except for the lanky tomcat, who sat golden and lordly among the garden's catnip and lemon balm. He turned his almond-shaped green eyes coolly on Houdini, who gave one of his funny un-cat-like bleats and tried to burrow fast and furious under Jill's thick hair.

"Never mind, Alexander," she told him, easing the kitten off her shoulder and into her arms. "He'll get used to you."

"Wah-wuh-WAH!" exclaimed Houdini from the safety of Jill's arms as she carried him inside. He jumped up on the wide barn-board windowsill and scanned the yard apprehensively. The red tabby gave him glance for glance, only leaving his post when Jill went out with milk and scraps for the outdoor cats. Alexander wove in and out around the girl's ankles, looking up every now and then to throw a disdainful look the newcomer's way. Houdini, secure in the knowledge that the older cat couldn't get at him on the porch, told him off in a series of long, drawn-out, bitter miaows.

Alexander actually came around sooner than Jill—or anyone else familiar with the red tabby's imperious ways—expected. He still occasionally chas ed Houdini every time he came upon him playing in the garden, snarling, hissing, and sometimes even cuffing him lightly when Jill was busy playing with the other cats and kittens or working on her elaborate moss gardens over by the lilac bushes in the side yard. But for the most part, Alexander let the kitten alone once he'd gotten it properly boxed into his little Siamese head that the red tabby ruled the yard. That meant that

Alexander got the best grasshoppers, mice, and moles (once, Houdini had seen him try to snatch a freshly killed mole from his chief mate, Sandy, a plump light-gray cat with a soft, orangy tinge to her fur); furthermore, he was to always have first pick of the females in season.

Houdini was still much too young to care about courtship rituals. He wasn't much of a hunter at this point either, for he'd been taken from his mother before she'd been able to teach him the finer points of stalking, pouncing, and playing with his prey. So he and Alexander got along decently enough in their own rough-around-the-edges way. And, once in awhile, when Jill gave them all a new catnip mouse to play with, the red tabby would casually toss it over to Houdini once he was done licking it and batting it about. But he could still send the little Siamese tearing across the yard, all puffer-tailed and screaming demon-cattishly just by giving him one of those long, cold, menacing looks of his.

Houdini lived with the other cats out in the tool shed now. He missed being with Jill all the time, even though she brought them all into the house as often as she could. Alexander, Houdini quickly learned, considered Jill his particular person: he waited with her at the bus stop every morning and made sure that he was sitting at attention on the far end of the low rock wall alongside the driveway when she came walking up it every afternoon. And he'd climb the front screen door when she was home, miaowing his most haunting miaow till she let him in.

Now Houdini was a dilute Siamese (Flame points, as Jill learned from a cat magazine, were the result of breeders putting Siamese with red tabbies), not one of the "primary" or original types; and, like most dilutes, he tended to be mellower in temperament than the Lilac, Chocolate, Blue, and Seal points; but he was Siamese enough not to suffer in silence. Occasionally, he'd beat Alexander to the front step; that much accomplished, he'd hook his claws into the wire mesh and, head tilted appealingly to the side, let loose a truly heart-rending "Wah-wuh!," sounding like the most abandoned of kittens. Sometimes, granted, he overplayed the part a bit, climbing to the very top of the door, then, suddenly fearful and unsure of his footing, he'd freeze, and Jill would have to get her dad or one of her three brothers to get him down again.

Mr. Leonard wasn't thrilled about the screen-climbing—Alexander, of course, had been at it for years, and now Dimity and Juliet were getting in on the act as well as Houdini—but he really liked the little cat with the loud miaow and nicknamed him "Dirty Harry" because he was always poking around among all the oil cans, old tools, and odds and ends of machinery in the shed and coming out more smudge-point than Flame point. The Siamese was always the first to greet Mr. Leonard whenever he went in there in search of a tool or some gizmo, stretching out a long, decidedly gray-tinged–reddish-gold paw and hooking it into the front of the man's jacket. "Trying to get around me, huh, you little scoundrel?" Jill's father would chuckle, reaching up to scritch the kitten's ears. And Houdini, his face Very Serious as usual and his eyes very round and un-Siamese-looking, would nuzzle him back ecstatically as if he was an especially delicious catnip mouse. Jill and the other Leonards had caught the two of them in this little "kissy-face" act often enough that nobody paid much attention to all his mutterings about "those damned cats ruining the screens" all that seriously.

Houdini loved Mr. Leonard and Jill—he loved his Juliet and Dimity and the Great Adventures they had in the big yard and out in the even bigger field—but he was only really completely satisfied when he was inside, getting extra petting and fussing from his girl. Outside, there were so many other cats miaowing for her attention, darting in and out between her ankles . . . so many that some days, she was pretty hard put to keep from tripping over them all when she was carrying their food out to the tool shed.

Inside—since just one cat came in for a visit at a time, generally—he could pretend that he was The One and Only, something that was very satisfying to his Siamese soul. He would lie curled up on Jill's chest while she was stretched out on her bed, reading, and he'd purr for the both of them—a good, loud crackling purr that practically drowned out the music on her radio. And when she wasn't reading, she'd fool with him, dragging some of her mother's crocheting yarn around the floor for him to chase or tossing a crumpled-up piece of paper in the air for him to catch. Sometimes he'd knock over her wastebasket when he thought she wasn't looking and rummage around for Good Stuff to Chase all on his own.

She gave him cold cuts or any slivers of turkey or chicken she happened to come across in the fridge. And he'd be right there next to her, close as he could possibly get without getting his head stuck in that big cold box where the humans kept their kill, standing up on his hind legs, pawing her leg anxiously. . . . Meals, as Houdini knew all too well from his days of abandonment, weren't Things a Kitten Could Take for Granted; and even now that his ivory-colored sides were sleek and glossy from regular feedings, he didn't turn his nose up at any fringe food benefits.

Nor did he have a problem with helping himself. Any food left out on the counter when he was around was fair game, he figured, even if it was only a bowl of cereal and milk. (The milk, he personally thought, tasted much better—all lovely and sugary—once the cereal had been sitting in it for awhile.) Once, Houdini wandered into the kitchen while Mr. Leonard was emptying the kill-box (there was a problem with one of the refrigerator coils). He caught a whiff of cold chicken and tried to scramble over the man's knees and squeeze his way in, explaining in loud, bleating "mer-rows" how Terribly Hungry he was. Mr. Leonard pushed the Siamese away, but his hands were gentle. "Get outta here, you bandit," he said, grinning in spite of himself. Houdini rubbed against him, burbling ecstatically. When that didn't produce the desired result, the kitten seized the man's hand between his front paws and gave it a nip. Not a full-fledged bite, mind you—just a little reminder.

"Hey!" yelped Mr. Leonard. "What the hell do you think you're doing?" Houdini stared up at him, looking like some angelic Valentine kitten with those huge blue eyes and that pink nose. Mr. Leonard had to laugh. "One minute, you're making love to me—the next, you're trying to take a bite outta me." Still, laughing, he shook his head and went back to his project.

Houdini bided his time. As soon as Jill's father headed downstairs for a tool, absent-mindedly leaving the refrigerator door slightly ajar, the kitten made a lunge for the unsuspecting plate of chicken. The drumstick never had a chance. He was still parading around the kitchen with it, proud as Alexander with a fresh kill, when Mr. Leonard came upstairs and wrestled it away from him despite his growls. How could the man do this to him? the kitten wondered. After all, he'd caught it all by himself, hadn't he? Houdini stalked angrily off to the living room and sat himself in the doorway with his back to Mr. Leonard, glancing over his furry shoulder every so often to see how the latter was taking it.

But when the man came in to take a short rest on the sofa a little later, Houdini hopped up alongside him and decided to forgive him. Humans just didn't understand about kill, he reasoned, as Mr. Leonard reached down to pat him. In fact, the Siamese suspected that they didn't even do their own kills: he'd seen them pull it out of those big brown paper bags (which were wonderful in themselves, making great caves to rattle around in), all wrapped up in that terrible-tasting clear stuff. And, anyway, he liked the man. A lot. He was fond of Jill's mother and brothers, too, and would've liked to have spent more time indoors with all of them.

But outside was good, too. The Leonards' yard was a large sprawling one, with plenty of secret cat places around it and still more down in the adjoining field for him to explore. The older cats, Sandy and Puff, kept close to Alexander and didn't take much notice of Houdini; but the other kittens regarded him as their leader, and the Flame point kitten gloried in his newfound importance.

Juliet and Dimity were best buddies with him now. Dimity was a shy but affectionate clown of a cat who often forgot to pull her tongue back in after giving herself baths; she'd just sit there for minutes at a time with the tip of it hanging out, making her look absurdly like Mr. Lion, one of Jill's old stuffed animals that Houdini enjoyed dragging around and kicking the stuffing (literally) out of during his visits inside. Juliet was very plump and very vain about her long, thick tigery coat, grabbing possessively at the cat comb and purring up a storm whenever Jill groomed her. Houdini especially adored the long-haired kitten, and she knew it. She'd go and rub up against him while he was eating and manage to nudge him away from the big food dish before he even knew what was happening. And he'd just sit there, watching her with goofy-eyed adoration while she chowed down on his share of the kibble.

One afternoon, she coaxed him into the woods beyond the field. Houdini had never ventured so far before; excited to the trembling tips of his whiskers, he ran up to practically every Scotch Pine, Blue Spruce, and birch tree, sharpening his claws or rubbing his face against their trunks and marking them for his own. Juliet did not wait for him but padded on determinedly. Houdini tore after her, the fallen leaves and needles crackling and crunching under his eager paws. He skidded to stop by a scrawny, twisted white birch. Juliet was there, all right, but so was this odd little black animal with a wide white stripe down its back and the fattest, fluffiest tail he'd ever seen trailing after it.

Houdini sniffed the air and wrinkled his nose. The creature was about the size of a very young kitten, but it had a strangely shaped head and a wild, pungent smell that no proper kitten would have. And it didn't hiss or spit or puff out its tail more or do any of the things that he or Juliet or Dimity would've done in its place. No, it just stood its ground, its little night-dark eyes peering out at them, unafraid. Houdini gave the air a second sniff; some instinct made him draw back, his tail all bottle-brushy.

Just then, Jill, who'd been combing the field for them, stepped out from behind a stand of pines. She took one look at the baby skunk and blanched. Stepping quietly, placing her weight on her toes instead of on her heels (the way her buddy Timmy Fitzgerald had taught her to do when they played Indians) and scarcely daring to breathe, she scooped Juliet up into her arms. She turned in Houdini's direction, but the skunk was too quick for her. It turned tail and blasted the young Siamese full in the face before disappearing into a thicket.

Unfortunately, Houdini had been grimacing at the time of the blast and had taken a direct hit to the mouth. The taste was foul beyond anything he'd ever experienced before, burning the inside of his throat and churning everything around in his stomach; he turned just as an already gagging Jill came up behind him and promptly threw up on her sneakers.

Groaning, the girl grabbed him with her free hand and carted both kittens home, where her dad helped her give them tomato-juice baths. Juliet finally jumped tub and waddled indignantly off, her lovely coat still dripping and plastered against her stocky little body. Houdini bore with the scrubbing and the tomato juice as bravely and nobly as he could, understanding in his own way that the humans were just doing what they could to get that Terrible Smell off him. And he even let Jill swaddle him up in an old ratty towel like a doll-baby and hold him like that till his fur dried. This part wasn't so bad, he decided, blinking up at her and doing push-me-pull-you's with his claws through the terrycloth. He snuggled up against her, sometimes purring at her closeness . . . sometimes nattering away about His Awful Experience and That Nasty Skunk-Thing. He didn't want to make Too Much of It, he assured her, but He had been Very Brave, hadn't he?

It wasn't altogether the happy ending that Houdini had been hoping for, however: Jill's dad declared the house out-of-bounds for the two kittens until they were, in his words, "thoroughly fumigated." Mr. Leonard had an unusually acute sense of smell from his days of working in his own father's slaughterhouse, and he was sure they'd miss a spot on

Houdini. And, indeed, they had—a tiny patch on the top of his head. So Juliet and Houdini were both kitties non gratis for a few weeks. The long-haired kitten didn't care overly much: she was fond of the humans, of course, but there were plenty of fun things for a kitten to do outside. Houdini, on the other hand, minded terribly, especially when he had to sit out by the porch steps and watch Jill cart Alexander in for a visit. The jealousy he felt was almost more than his little Siamese heart could take. And the long-bodied–red-gold tabby always seemed to be smirking at him from over the girl's shoulder.

Houdini might spend most of his time with Juliet and Dimity, but he also liked running races across the field with Cassandra and Daphne, who were almost full-grown. Cassandra was a shy, slender golden-brown tiger with velvety white paws who moved with quicksilver grace among the long-tall, rustling field grasses. Daphne was an impish white cat with dark-gray tiger patches and round gold eyes. She had never flown one of those winged beasts, as Houdini had, but she'd ridden in the car back from Mrs. Leonard's parents' farm and definitely liked it. She was forever sneaking off in Jill's oldest brother's car, and Lee was forever having to drive back to his friends' houses to retrieve her. "Nobody ever told me I was gonna have to be some cat's personal chauffeur," he used to groan every time he brought her back; but his hands were always very gentle as he handed "some cat" back to his kid sister, and he never refused to go get her either.

It was Daphne who discovered the hole in the floorboard of Mr. Leonard's old car. It had been a warm fall, mellow as the sun on the red, yellow, and orange-brown leaves; but the leaves were all gone now, and the weather was bitterly cold, even for November. Houdini longed in his bones for the warmth of Jill's room with all its kid clutter (some of which made great noises when he nudged it off the shelves) and the kneadable green-yellow-and-white-striped afghan on her bed. The cats couldn't go into the house without Jill to watch them—that was another one of The Rules—and the hours that she was at school seemed longer than ever as they waited in the tool shed or out by the back steps for her to come hurrying up the driveway to them. Jill did her best for her cat-friends: she got a hold of a couple of big cardboard cartons and lined them with ratty old sweaters and other cast-off clothing. And Mr. Leonard picked up some hay from the farm for the boxes as well. It had a wonderful sweet smell to it, and the kittens loved diving into it. And it did keep them all warmer, no doubt about it; but the nattering, fur-ruffling wind still managed to sneak through the wider chinks between the boards of the shed walls, biting right through to the bone.

One afternoon, the wind picked up and turned so evil—a wicked, slashing wind—that Houdini, Juliet, Dimity, and Cassandra gave up stalking each other through the crackly dead leaves and huddled together by the dryer vent. The vent was sending out some wonderful blasts of hot air, and the younger cats sent out a collective squunk of relief. It wasn't as good as being in the nice, warm house, of course, but those blasts did take the edge off the wind. Anyway, Jill would be home from school soon—Houdini knew that much from his inner clock—and maybe, just maybe she would be able to let them all onto the big back porch. He gently kneaded his claws against Dimity's calico side—she had such lovely plushy fur—at the thought. Then, suddenly, he caught sight of Daphne slipping out from under the spruce hedge and darting toward the brown car. Houdini shook off Juliet, who had been gracefully sprawled across his back and sat up, forgetting the cold in his curiosity. His blue eyes narrowed thoughtfully as he watched Daphne scoot under the car and vanish from sight.

There was no resting for him after that, of course. He trotted over in the direction of the car. The three females trailed after him, their own curiosity set in motion. Houdini poked his head under the car. No Daphne. He ventured a little further underneath. Still no Daphne. Then he spied the rusted-out hole in the bottom of the car, towards the front. He ambled over to it and checked out the hole; then, raising himself ever so slightly on his hind legs, he stuck his head in. He still didn't see Daphne, but her scent was very strong near the bottom of the front seat. He wriggled his way up into the car and climbed over the seat in pursuit. And there, on the back-seat shelf was Daphne, stretched out in all of her two-toned glory, looking almost too pleased with herself to purr.

Houdini jumped up and touched his pink nose to hers in greeting. She batted him playfully with her paw but moved over a bit to make room for him. Pretty soon, Juliet, Dimity, and Cassandra came climbing over the back of the seat, too. There wasn't room for them all, of course—only plump prima donna-ish Juliet managed to somehow squeeze herself up there, right between Houdini and Daphne—but Dimity and Cassandra made themselves more than comfortable on the back seat itself.

They were all still sacked out in the old brown clunker when Jill came home. The three shelf kitties sat up at the sound of her footsteps coming up the driveway; the other two cats, startled by the commotion over their heads, roused themselves from their snooze and stood up on their hind legs, peering out one of the side windows. Jill grinned when she saw it and ran in to coax Lee into taking a picture of it with his camera. Of course, by the time they made it back out, Dimity and Cassandra, the shyest and most easily startled of the bunch, had bolted for the safety of the tool shed. But Houdini, Juliet, and Daphne mugged for the camera for all they were worth.

From then on, the younger cats regarded Mr. Leonard's beat-up old car as their own particular property. Alexander, Sandy, and Puff were more leery of it and kept their distance. That was fine, as far as Houdini was concerned. He liked having the upper paw over Alexander for once. As for Jill's family . . . well, Mr. Leonard sometimes complained about how much longer it took him to make what should've been just a simple trip downtown, "havin' to do a damn cat check" every time. But the corners of his mouth always twitched the tiniest bit, as if he was almost as much amused by the "car kitties" as Jill was.

IV

The February sun was working its way through the cracked, dirt-streaked shed windows, spilling itself onto the brick floor. Sandy was curled up on top of an antique, pot-bellied cast-iron stove that Jill's dad hadn't quite figured out what to do with. Puff was napping alongside Cassandra (who, along with the older matronly Sandy, was one of the few survivors of the old white cat's many litters) in a big carton under the window that looked out on to the spruce hedge. Dimity and Juliet were up in the rafters, sprawled out on some warped boards and an old door that Mr. Leonard had stowed up there because his pack-rat soul simply couldn't bear the idea of scrapping it. The cats had gleefully taken over the makeshift loft, which gave them a prime spot for spying down on any human being entering the shed without being easily observed themselves. And Alexander sat regally among the old tools, coils of rope and wire, dented aluminum pitchers, and spigot-less watering cans on the wide shelf by the door, his long striped tail twitching impatiently.

Houdini was perched on a rusted-shut milk can below the shelf, but not so near it that Alexander could jump him easily. Like his rival, he had his eyes glued to the door as he waited for Jill to come in with their afternoon meal. Usually, this was Houdini's favorite time of day. He'd stand on his hind legs and, grabbing her leg with his front paws, do a little dance for her until she'd put the food down for them. And afterwards, Jill would sit down on the lop-sided iron milking-stool and play with them until she had to go in and do her homework or chores. The shed would be crackling with the sound of the cats' purring as they scurried over to her for attention or began washing up from their feed.

But today Houdini felt restless. A sadness tugged at him—a sense of loss the like of which he hadn't felt since he'd been abandoned by his first humans. Like most Siamese and Abyssinians, he was extremely sensitive to changes in his environment, and this was no minor one. Daphne had not been seen by any of them for days now; and while Houdini wasn't as close to her as he was to Juliet and Dimity, in his own way he missed the friendly, graceful cat with her sense of adventure. He even wandered far into the woods looking for her one afternoon—he'd often seen her coming from that direction with her latest kill—but there'd been nothing there, not even tufts of her bi-colored fur clinging to the tangled trumpet vine and bittersweet.

The old storm door creaked open just then. It was Jill, of course, carrying a milk carton and a big bag of dry cat food. Houdini leaped down from the old milk can and hurried over to her, rubbing himself anxiously against her ankles. Jill stooped down to pet him, but her touch had a listlessness that he didn't remember ever feeling in it before. She turned abruptly away in mid-pat—also unusual for her—and began filling the bowls and pie tins. The other cats came spilling out of the box and down from the rafters. Even Alexander forgot his dignity as Czar-Cat enough to come leaping down from his perch and dance around Jill on his hind legs, hooking his front claws gently into the worn denim of her jeans leg. She laughed as she carefully unhooked his claws, but it was a short, empty laugh.

Houdini 37

She plunked herself down on her grandfather's old milking-stool, her eyes sad and tired with too much looking for a slender white-and-tiger barn cat whose face was so comical, just looking at her made you smile. Daphne, like Juliet, had come from the farm; and right from the beginning, she'd been a sociable, affectionate character, not skittish the way most barn cats were. She'd come up to Jill one morning, while the latter was reading by the big rock in the side yard and just curled up alongside her and started burbling away. From then on, the little cat had always seemed to know when Jill would be there and would wait by the rock or under the nearby hydrangea with its bridal bloom. And she'd follow her around the barnyard or down the lane to the pond. Finally, Mr. Leonard had yielded to Jill's coaxing and said OK, what difference did one more mouth make, but this was the last one, she couldn't have every cat she saw. (This had been about a month or so before Houdini had made his historic flight back home from the wedding with them.) And Daphne had ridden home with them, utterly at her ease, purring and watching the passing roadsides. A queen on a royal progress....

Lost in remembering, Jill started as Houdini jumped into her lap, then put her arm around him, resting her cheek against him. He'd grown a lot since they'd gotten him: he had the stockier build of a red tabby, not the tapering one of a Siamese, and he was as comforting as a big, squeezable teddy bear. Alexander, too, came away from the food dish and sat down next to the stool, butting his head worriedly against her hand.

She stroked both toms until the sadness let loose its hold on her somewhat. They had always been far more affectionate than her female cats. Except for Daphne, Jill reminded herself, and the pain stabbed her again, paper-cut-thin and ever-widening.... She'd been combing the fields for Daphne, knowing all along that the cat wasn't there most likely, that she'd probably gone off in Dad's or Lee's car again, and that they just hadn't realized it in enough time to turn back and find her. *I hope somebody took her in and gave her a good home,* the girl thought drearily. Not much comfort, but it was the best she could summon up at that moment. This was the worst of it, the not-knowing. Horrible as it is to get off the school bus and see your cat or kitten lying crushed in the road (and she'd seen that plenty, too, what with the cats living outdoors and their house being on a major route), at least you didn't sit around imagining the poor thing out in the woods, cold and starving and maybe even too injured to move, let alone hunt....

She gave Houdini and Alexander another pat apiece. Then, easing the younger cat off her lap, she got up and slowly looked around her. She walked over to the shelves at the back of the shed—part of the "stairway" that the cats used to get to their loft—and winced as she caught sight of the old, braided chair mat on the middle one. Lying on it was a rose-pink yam hair-ribbon. Daphne had staked her claim on both items: the mat was covered with loose white and tiger fur, and the ribbon was more knots than ribbon, Jill had had to tie it together so many times from the young cat savaging it.

She picked up the ribbon now, letting it slide though her hands onto the brick floor. Like the be-furred blue-and-copper mat with its braid coming undone, it suddenly seemed like so much trash. She should probably just throw them both away.

"Mr-row?" She glanced down, and there was Houdini gazing up at her, his blue eyes questioning. She bent down and, picking him up, laid him against her shoulder. "Hey,

Dirty Harry," she said softly, using her dad's name for him. She fluffed the satiny white fur around his ears and neck. He licked her face in return, then, carried away by his affection for her, gave her nose a playful nip. "Ouch!" Jill yelped. But she couldn't help laughing, the Siamese's expression was so comical. Like Daphne's, she suddenly thought.

She loosened his paws from around her neck and set him down on the braided mat. The blue and copper tones, faded as they were, deepened his blue eyes and reddish-gold markings. "This is yours now," she told Houdini, who tucked his front paws under him and touched his pink nose to hers. She picked up the bedraggled piece of yarn and stuffed it in her pocket . . . but not to throw away later on.

She glanced around the shed one more time, then walked sadly out, the old, creaking storm door shut behind her.

Houdini didn't forget Daphne entirely. But her image faded in his memory, just as the winter with its slushy, brownish snow faded into spring. There were grasshoppers and mice to chase down in the field, and herbs and flowers to check out as they pushed their way through the earth. He and Juliet spent one satisfying morning digging up some new plants that Mrs. Leonard had just put in, chewing holes in the mauve sweater she'd left out on the garden bench for good measure. They explored the field and the woods more thoroughly than they had in their kittenhood. And when Juliet came into season that May, they mated.

Juliet waddled though the long, warm late-spring and summer days—looking, Kathy Dewey, her friend next door, giggled, like a pregnant water buffalo. In the cool of the early morning, Houdini would go off on his own; his hunting skills had improved greatly, and he often brought back a mole or a field mouse for his Juliet. Patiently, ignoring his own hunger—there was nothing like a good hunt to sharpen it—he stood guard, making sure that none of the other cats tried to steal his gift away from her. Sometimes he would bathe her. Her scent was different now, bringing back shadowy memories of his kittenhood and the warm milkiness that had been his mother.

One July morning, Houdini woke up to find Juliet gone from the new box that Jill had set up for her in the shed. He sniffed the hay where she'd been sleeping; her scent was still there but was starting to grow cold. So she'd been gone for a couple of hours maybe. He stretched and hopped out of the box. Puff and Sandy, worn out from nursing their new litters, blinked sleepy green eyes at him from the larger cardboard carton, where they'd set up their own communal nursery. The other females, tired from hunting and playing tag in the field the night before, didn't even do that much. Houdini moseyed over to the cat door, narrowly missing a half-playful, half-bossy swipe from Alexander's paw—the older tom was stretched out on the lower tool shelf, one white-gloved paw dangling over the edge—and squeezed his comfortable bulk through.

It was early yet. The air was still cool and the sky still awash with splashes of rose, peach, and gold. He followed Juliet's trail through the dew-spattered grass across the backyard, past the lilac bushes and Jill's moss gardens, and into the side yard, where they often hunted for grasshoppers. But the scent didn't let up there. Past the giant hemlock trees and the rusted grass-bound cultivator, he trotted until he came to the narrow wildflower-starred strip that separated the Leonards' land from their neighbors'. Houdini seldom ventured this far, although Alexander was notorious for his frequent raids on the Deweys' garbage cans over by the old barn-turned-garage. He had even been known to bring his own offspring along with him.

Faint mewlings tickled Houdini's ears now as he neared the grove of spruce and pine trees that shadowed the Deweys' house. He picked up his pace. There, in a hollowed-out log, he found Juliet surrounded by five sturdy kittens. Houdini approached cautiously, not sure what to make of this new development or what his reception would be. Mild-mannered Puff had hissed at him when he'd tried to check out her kittens too closely, and Sandy, infinitely less mild-mannered, had once given him a sharp claw to the nose.

But Juliet showed none of their touchiness. She touched her little pink nose to his and purred proudly. Houdini nuzzled her back and sat down, his head cocked to one side as he watched the kittens nurse, their tiny claws working in and out of Juliet's long white belly fur. He put a curious paw out, then quickly drew it back. But the cries of one little tortoiseshell who'd gotten pushed away from the nipple she'd been feeding from attracted his attention, and he moved closer. He sniffed his tiny daughter thoughtfully, and caught not only Juliet's comfortable milk-and-hay scent, but something of his own scent as well. He lay down alongside the log, his paws kneading the grass and clover beneath them as if he, too, was a kitten. Later, they would move the kittens to the shed, away from the foxes, hawks, and hoot owls that came up from the dark, dark woods beyond the field to do their night-hunting. For now, he was content to watch over his new brood, his purr burbling away in the breezy after-dawn.

Houdini took being a father-cat very seriously, unlike Alexander, who rarely condescended to notice the little red-tabby and multi-colored kittens that were toddling after him as soon as they could put one paw in front of the other. Houdini—or "Papa Harry," as Jill and her brothers took to calling him—loved boxing with his sons and daughters and swishing his long tail about for them to pounce on. He washed them as thoroughly as Juliet did, and, once they were weaned, probably spent more time with them, for she quickly tired of motherhood and took to hanging out at the neighbors'. The Deweys might not care for Alexander and his trash-picking, but they grew increasingly fond of the pretty tiger cat and often let her into their kitchen for snacks. Dimity took to following her friend over and found herself equally welcome, for the Deweys had just lost their beautiful Maltese cat, Elsa, and hadn't had the heart to go looking for another one just yet. The two female cats grew to like the kitchen, where there was no competition from others of their kind—they even got used to Honeybird, the Deweys' golden retriever, who used to cradle them close in her great front paws and bathe them with her big sloppy tongue—and came home less and less.

In early September, when the field-grasses began turning golden-brown and the field itself was blue with chicory where it wasn't yellow and orange with the puckered-up petals of butter-and-eggs, distemper struck. All of Sandy's and Puff's kittens caught it and died. Sandy herself, the feisty little mother-cat that she was, grew lank, dull-eyed, and listless before disappearing into the woods beyond the field forever.

Juliet's offspring were sturdy and thrifty enough kittens to fight off the disease; but there were other dangers that Houdini couldn't fend off for them, try as he did. One dark-gray tiger kitten, Kali, wandered off into the field on a cold fall night. Jill and Kathy were just getting ready to organize a search party the next morning when they caught sight of the kitten toddling weakly down the lane by the Deweys' barn.

"There she is!" shouted Kathy, whose eyes were a lot sharper than her friend's, and they ran toward her.

Jill got to Kali first and was just about to scoop her up in her glad hands when she saw why the kitten was so wobbly-pawed. Blood was spilling out of a good-sized hole in Kali's stomach, splashing on the grass and wild white-clover blossoms. They could even see some of her insides (Jill's own insides did a few roller-coaster swerves and dives when she realized what she was staring at), looking like they were about to fall out onto the ground like stuffing out of a ripped sofa cushion. Some wild animal must've found her alone in the field and savaged her; it was a miracle that she was even alive. Jill rose unsteadily to her feet, almost backed into Kathy, who was coming up behind her, and blurted out what she'd seen. The younger blonde-haired girl bent down just enough to get a reasonably good look and gagged. They shrank away from Kali, who kept weaving determinedly toward them, certain in her kitten way that these humans she trusted would be able to make her terrible pain go away.

Finally, Kathy bolted inside and called her parents' vet, who sent a lab tech out to pick up the kitten. Kali could not be saved, he told the children as kindly as he could: he could tell just by a quick examination that she'd lost a lot of blood, and, anyway, the risk of her having picked up rabies from whatever wild animal had attacked her was too great.

"Sweetheart, I'm sorry you had to see it" was all Mr. Leonard said when he came home from work and heard the story. Jill was sorry, too. And she was even sorrier that next week, when the bill for putting Kali down came from Dr. Northrop's office. Dad never complained about the bill in her hearing, but she knew that there simply wasn't enough money for trips to the vet's and the like. If the cats were really sick, Mr. Leonard usually put them down himself as quickly and quietly as possible.

So Jill tried to make up for that additional expense by finding homes for the rest of Juliet's kittens. She gave the two fattest and fluffiest ones—real Victorian chocolate-box kittens—away to a boy in her Sunday school class, even though Scott got mad at her for "giving away the best ones." *Two down, two to go*, she told herself, although she hated the idea of giving away Sassy (short for Sarsaparilla) and Peri (short for Periwinkle), who were her favorites from this litter. But she made herself ask Patty, the only other girl in the class, if she'd be interested in one or both of them. *Please say no*, she prayed, crossing her fingers hard.

"Oh, that would be neat!" Patty exclaimed. Jill's heart did a nose-dive: she could feel the corners of her mouth drooping despite her efforts to be brave about it. But the other girl evidently didn't see it and went on copying over the questions for their weekly homework assignment in that flowery handwriting of hers that Jill envied but couldn't imitate. "I'd really like one. But I'd only want it as a kitten. I'd give it back to you when it grew up."

Jill laid down her pen and stared. She loved kittens, too, of course; but nothing and nobody could ever have persuaded her to give up Alexander, Houdini, Cassandra, Dimity, and Juliet. Kittens were—well, so full of themselves, as Timmy said, you couldn't really make friends with them like you could with older cats. "I couldn't do that," she said finally. "It wouldn't be fair to the cat." Patty gave her a blank look, shrugged, and turned away. Jill bit back a sigh and went back to scribbling down the rest of the assignment from the board. *Well, I tried*, she argued with herself. *And anyhow, I found a home for the two boy kittens.* That's two more than Mom and Dad expected me to give away.

V

Houdini crouched by the outside dryer vent, letting the heat fluff out his coat, which had thickened with the coming of winter. The Siamese was doubly glad he'd been able to claim this spot. A lot of times, he had to fight Alexander for it, and he almost always lost the battles: today, however, the red tabby had gone down to the field to hunt, his tail waving long and coppery against the frost-tipped grasses and brittle dead wood-aster stalks. Houdini tucked his big front paws under his chest and worked on a purr, but it was a wheezy half-hearted one at best.

Truth was, he was lonely, almost as lonely as he'd been back in the on-campus apartment with only the kitten-in-the-glass for company. Juliet and Dimity practically lived at the Deweys' now, divvying their time up between the kitchen and the empty hayloft up in the old barn. Houdini had wandered over there with them a few times. But he was terrified of Honeybird and Solana, the high-spirited puppy that the Deweys had just acquired. Besides, he belonged here. Where his girl was. It was as simple as that.

So he roamed the field and woods by himself most days. And spent as much time as he was allowed inside with Jill, sensing her sadness at Juliet's and Dimity's defections. Puff, too, was gone, old age and breast cancer having finally claimed her, and it was downright eerie not seeing the thin white cat patrolling the yard, an army of kittens tagging along behind her. Alexander, Cassandra, and the two surviving kittens took the changes pretty much in their furry stride, but neither Houdini nor Jill could.

Cassandra came strolling over to the dryer vent just then. Houdini looked up and blinked his blue eyes affectionately; they touched noses, and he made room for her, then began washing the top of her golden-brown head. Cassandra was all that was left of his original group of playmates, and he'd become especially fond of the shy little tiger cat. But, like most Siamese, he tended to be loyal to one mate. But he was deprived of her, he moped.

Houdini gave Cassandra a final lick. He got up and stretched, the wind teasing his fur unmercifully. Then he caught sight of Alexander strolling past the tool shed, heading their way. Not anxious for a fight, Houdini exited stage left. He sat in the middle of the driveway, glancing around him and pondering his next move. The November sky had turned a lovely watered-silk blue-and-gold. Jill would be home soon. But it was too chilly to wait out here in the open, what with the wind picking up and all. He glanced over at Mr. Leonard's car. Not quite as cozy as his little nook by the dryer vent, but at least he'd have some shelter from the wind there.

Houdini sauntered over to the car, trying to keep track of Alexander out of the corner of his eye. Mustn't let the older cat smell his fear. Once he'd reached his destination, he quickly jumped through the hole in the floorboard and curled up on the back seat. Mr. Leonard hadn't been home that long, so the car was still fairly warm. Some of Juliet's scent still lingered, too, even though she didn't hang out there very often now, and it made him feel less lonely for her . . . almost as though she was there, snuggled up against him. He tucked his front paws back under his chest and went to sleep.

Houdini awoke to darkness. He could feel the car growling and sputtering beneath his paws. He crouched low in the back, so quiet with fear, Mr. Leonard never even guessed that he was there. After awhile, the car stopped, and Houdini heard Jill's father open the door and get out. Unsure, the cat waited a few seconds, then made for the front seat. He ducked down the hole and out from under the car, only to find himself not in his own backyard but in a poorly lit parking lot. He was just about to head back to the car when some tall gangly boys came out of the drugstore. Their noise frightened him; then one of them saw the strange white cat peering out at them from the darkness and threw a bottle at him. The bottle missed Houdini, but the sound of glass shattering against the hardtop sent him running past the Salvation Army box and under a nearby hedge. He crouched there in the shadows, waiting for their footsteps to die away.

Even then, he bided his time, just in case any of them might decide to come back. He was not used to overt cruelty—his first humans had abandoned him, yes, but that had been an indifferent, unthinking kind of cruelty, not vicious and deliberate like this—and he wasn't sure what to expect next from these boys, who were so different from Jill's brothers or her friend, Timmy. *They're like foxes or weasels*, he thought. *Scary. Can't tell what they're going to do next. Better to lie low for awhile.* Finally, he stepped out from his hiding place and ventured back into the parking lot. But the old brown car was gone.

He waited there for a long time, waiting for Mr. Leonard to find him, just as somebody had always managed to find him whenever he'd gotten himself lost in the field or stuck up in one of the huge maple trees in the backyard before. This time, though, nobody came. A sharp, unfriendly wind whipped through Houdini's fur, and he shivered, remembering the shed ... Cassandra's shimmery pussywillow-soft fur against his face ... the tickly warmth of the hay in the boxes ... hay. He caught a whiff of it and of cats and other animals not far from him at all. He trotted off in that direction, his stomach bothering him more than a little. It was long past time for his afternoon meal.

The town where the Leonards lived had once been a farming community. And although a number of small shops and businesses had elbowed their way in, there were still quite a few dairy farms on the outskirts, where Houdini found himself now. He wasn't really all that far from his home, but it might have been a galaxy away for all he knew.

The road became rougher and harder on his paw pads, and the smell from the cows and chickens was pretty pungent, even from a cat's point of view. After a little ways, a barn came into sight. Houdini hesitated, then moved cautiously past the gate into the barnyard, stepping daintily around the manure. Weaving about by the barn door, miaowing their hunger, were some of the scrawniest, goopiest-eyed cats Houdini had ever seen. A tall broad-shouldered man tossed meat scraps down into a couple of old pie tins. Then he picked up the bucket by his feet and poured some milk into a dirty white plastic dish that had once been the bottom half of a detergent jug.

Houdini, fearful of strangers after his encounter with the boys in the parking lot, waited for the man to go back into the house before he drew near the food. A tattered-eared red tabby, stockier than the others and blind in one eye, jumped him, tearing out a large hunk of white fur. Houdini broke away and hid behind a pile of boards and snarled-up barbed wire over by the chicken coop. Only when the warrior-cat finally slunk away into the night did Houdini come back out and stake a place for himself at the milk dish with a bunch of potbellied, scruffy kittens. The milk was dirty and had bits of straw floating about in it, but Houdini was past caring at that point. Afterwards, he checked out the scrap tins. There wasn't much left, just a bit bone and gristle, but he chewed on it till not even the ghost of its flavor was left.

He set up temporary headquarters at the dairy farm, snatching what food he could and taking care to keep a good amount of barnyard (and of pasture, too, sometimes) between himself and the tabby, whom he heard the farmer call "Old Red-Face." The man took little notice of the new cat on the scene except to comment casually to his wife one evening that there was "this funny-looking cat hanging around the barn. Something like the Siamese in that picture of yours, but the colors are all different, kinda reddish and white with these big blue eyes." One cat more or less didn't trouble him: they earned their keep by keeping the rats and mice down, and, in turn, distemper would thin out the group when it got too large. He wasn't an unkind man, but he honestly thought that he was doing enough for that ragtag bunch of cats in the barn by giving them shelter, scraps, and whatever milk was left over.

Houdini, for his part, steered clear of the farmer. After the bottle-throwing episode out in the parking lot, he was more than a little leery of human males. The farmer's wife, a big woman with dark hair and dangling earrings who dressed in gaillardia-bright colors, liked cats and often came out to the barn to fool with them. It was a regular feast day for them whenever she showed up, for she always brought good-sized slices of roast or pieces of chicken with the skin still hanging off them with her, and she talked to them and patted each one individually. After awhile, Houdini got used to her and found that he didn't mind her touching him. She was nice and kind, and her big hands were surprisingly gentle on his fur. He could tell that she meant well by him, so he even managed to work up a friendly little purr for her just to let her know How Much He Appreciated It.

In reality, though, Houdini spent little time at the farm. Most days saw him trotting up and down the wide, rough country road, listening for the spluttering engine of Mr. Leonard's old brown car. He even returned to the drugstore parking lot every other day or so in case it showed up again. He'd sit in front of the drugstore and wait, not understanding why neither Jill nor her father came for him. The lady at the little family-run grocery store next door took pity on him; she could tell he was a real pretty cat under all that soot and soil he'd gotten smeared with, and those blue eyes of his were just sweet. She began putting out cream and left-over sandwich meat from the luncheon counter for him.

Sometimes a restlessness came over Houdini, and he'd head up the other end of the road, past the farm. There were a lot of old clapboard houses and a big played-out old apple orchard up that way. And off by itself, on the other side of the road—keeping itself to itself, so to speak—was a small white cottage with mourning-dove-gray shutters and a red door. It, too, was old, though not as old as the gussied-up farmhouses that seemed bent on staring it down. In the cottage's front yard was an herb garden, full of catnip and lemon balm and other plants that made Houdini think of home with a yearning. Of course, they were all nothing but dried stalks and blossoms now, but enough of their summer scent lingered to make him remember. He kept heading back there time and again, rubbing his head against the winter-brittle stalks and even rolling kittenishly on the frozen ground.

The Siamese set off early one morning for the garden. There'd been an ice storm a couple of nights before, and he'd had to take cover in the hayloft in order to avoid Old Red-

Face and the sharp-hoofed cows. But the sun had finally fingered its way through this morning, melting much of the ice, and the ground, though cold and sodden, didn't feel quite so harsh on his sore paw pads.

Once he'd reached the cottage, he made his way over to a choice lilac bush, which was almost the size of a small tree, standing off to the side of the garden. His movements, stealthy as they were for so big a cat, scared off the six or seven cardinals who'd been roosting on its bare branches like so many flame-red blossoms. He pretended not to have noticed them and proceeded to sharpen his claws on the gnarly gray bark.

After one last good stretch-and-scratch, Houdini sat down on his haunches and glanced around him, trying to get the lay of this particular garden. There was a birdfeeder hanging off a clothesline pole a few feet away from the lilac bush. Finally, one of the cardinals, vivid as hope against the gray sky, decided to take a chance and flew over to it. His mate soon joined him. They fed with a dainty diligence, the male pausing now and again to offer her a sunflower seed. Houdini, half-starved on his lean diet of farm rations and luncheon-counter pickings, watched them with owl eyes; then he crouched down low, every muscle in him quivering.

He sprang. His paws hit the tray of the feeder, and the birds flew off to the cover of the trees again. Houdini fell back, landing smack in the patch of soggy picked-over seed. He quickly sat up and began to wash his shoulder to cover his embarrassment, just in case someone had seen him flub this one up. True, there didn't seem to be any other animals or humans outside; still, it was a matter of feline pride. A little extra washing never hurt, anyway.

But someone *had* seen him. Even as he worked over an imaginary smudge on his left front paw, his cat sense told him that there were eyes fixed on him. Slowly, cautiously, Houdini swiveled around until he was facing the front picture window. There, her wide face pushed against the glass, was a long-haired black cat, her plume of a tail puffed out even more and lashing against the glass.

Houdini sat there, one front paw raised hesitantly. He edged a little closer to the house, and the unknown cat's tail beat even harder against the window-pane. He knew that she couldn't get at him through the glass, but he decided to retreat, anyway. Besides, his stomach told him that it was about time for his morning snack down at the corner store. He turned and hurried down toward the road.

He'd just gotten to the edge of the long unpaved driveway when a large dog materialized from around the corner and made a bolt for him. Houdini panicked and dashed across the road, not seeing or hearing the car bearing down on them both. But he heard the screech of the brakes . . . felt the tire bear down on his front left paw, crushing it. . . .

VI

Grace Tyne, the artist who owned the cottage and the large black Persian, heard the screech just as she was stepping out of her front door to go run some errands. She dropped her keys and ran down to the foot of the driveway. A large white cat with reddish-gold markings was lying across the road. She thought his sides were moving but couldn't tell for sure from where she stood.

Grace darted across, her feet slip-sliding on the slush, and gently gathered the cat up. It was still breathing. Then she took the pale-green scarf from around her neck and wrapped as much of it around him as she could. She carried him into the house and laid him down on the couch, replacing the soggy, bloody scarf with a favorite old turquoise afghan that her grandmother had made her. They were on their way to the veterinary clinic as soon as she'd gotten through to them on the phone and found a carton large enough for the injured animal to travel in.

"Looks like he's got one helluva concussion," Dr. Mullen told Grace as he examined the cat. He was a short, stocky man with prematurely gray hair and glasses that were always sliding down the bridge of his nose. He pushed them up now and shook his head as he checked the crushed paw for the umpteenth time. "What worries me most, though, is that front leg." He saw her questioning look and nodded grimly. "We might have to amputate if those nerve endings are as badly damaged as I think they are."

"And if you don't?" Grace looked down at the cat, a world of pity stirring in her heart.

"Gangrene," the vet replied shortly. He took off his bifocals and rubbed them absent-mindedly against his lab coat, then pushed them back up his nose. "You sure you want to go through all this for a cat that isn't even yours, Grace?"

She shrugged. "I'd want somebody to do as much for my cats if they ever found themselves in this guy's predicament."

He chuckled. "Should've known." He stroked the cat's flanks. "I'll do what I can. You want me to alter him?"

"I guess so. He'll just fight with Lilah and Merlin otherwise. And you know Lilah, she doesn't take any prisoners." Grace bit her lip. Just one more expense she really didn't need on her slender income. Still, what else could she do? The cat deserved his chance. And she knew herself, she couldn't walk away without one very guilty conscience. "If I ever find his owners, I'll get them to pay me back."

"You have great faith," the older man said. He peered at her over his horn-rimmed glasses. "I'll give you a ring later today or early tomorrow morning and let you know how this fellow's doing."

It was early evening when Houdini came to. The strong antiseptic smells terrified him; so did the barking and whimpering from the dogs in the cages across the room. He could hear cats, too, crying out for their owners. His eyes gradually became more focused; he could just see the tip of a white-and-black paw reaching up from the cage below. He tried to miaow, but, for once in his short life, his voice failed him, and the stranger's paw disappeared back into her cage.

Houdini blinked and tried to reach out through the bars of his cage with his left front paw. But there was nothing. Just a neatly stitched stump where that paw should have been. And yet he still had feeling there, almost as if a ghost-paw had taken the place of his long reddish-gold one. He put his head down and lay in his cage, waiting for his humans, who, for some reason past his cat's understanding, still did not come for him.

───── ⌘⌘⌘ ─────

Grace brought Houdini back to her cottage a few days after his operation. She fixed up a place for him in the small downstairs bathroom, complete with litter box and the lovely warm afghan he'd ridden to and from the vet's in. It had some of his scent on it already, the artist reasoned. It would be the one semi-familiar thing in this strange new world of his.

She placed some dry food and water within easy reach of his bedding but not too close to the makeshift litter box. And she put a felt catnip mouse and a crocheted ball down for him, figuring they would give him something to bop around as soon as his strength came back to his remaining front paw.

Houdini nibbled at the food, feebly batted at the toys, and then sank down into the afghan's warmth. Grace sat down on the floor next to him and held her fingers out to him. Houdini sniffed them thoughtfully, then touched his nose briefly to them. She wasn't Jill, but there was a quiet gentleness about her movements that soothed him just then. He gave her fingers one more sniff—an approving one this time—and went to sleep.

He awoke to a scratching at the door. A gray-tabby paw was poking its way through the gap between it and the threshold. Houdini sat up, his blue eyes wide. The paw waggled at him. Slowly, he rose to his feet and toward the door. The paw vanished, then darted teasingly back into the room. Houdini's head moved quickly back and forth, his tail puffing out with excitement. He took a poke at the striped paw, but it kept disappearing and reappearing. *Enough is enough*, the Siamese decided. He pushed against the door till it gave way (like most of the doors in that old house, it was so warped, it didn't latch securely), and he found himself practically muzzle-to-muzzle with a gray tabby male, not much older than he was.

The strange cat opened his mouth in a soundless hiss. Houdini tilted his head to one side, then realized that the other cat was simply going through the feline ritual of introduction and meant him no harm. Besides, he didn't smell like a full-fledged, battle-ready tom. So Houdini crouched down and lowered his head to show that he understood whose territory this was. The tabby cuffed him lightly and stalked off, but not too far. He sat down by the kitchen table and watched Houdini with wide, friendly green eyes. *Want to play?* those eyes said.

I might, the Siamese telegraphed back. He sat up and began lightly touching up his fur, feeling a bit more like his old self. Definitely more at ease.

It was a short-lived ease, though. Just then, a low growl crackled through the kitchen. A long-haired black cat—the same one he'd glimpsed through the window the morning of his accident—stalked into the kitchen, and, she made it clear, was definitely ready for battle. She came at him now, a big, black whirlwind with her golden eyes ablaze. Houdini, forgetting his injury, tried to run back into the bathroom. He reeled, almost tumbling over himself. The black cat slunk towards him, belly low, his tail thwacking against the brick-patterned linoleum. She struck out at him, her claws scraping his left shoulder.

Houdini cried out in his shrill bleating way, more in anger at the she-cat's uppityness than in hurt. The woman came rushing into the kitchen from the next room. "Lilah!" she exclaimed, grabbing a squirt bottle from off the counter.

The black cat took one gander at that squirt bottle and fled through the open cellar door, her big double paws thumping down the sunken wooden steps. Grace put the bottle down on the floor and went straight over to Houdini. "Poor fella," she said, sitting down on the floor beside him and checking out the Persian's work. "You've had a time of it. Sorry Lilah's not more sociable."

She lifted him up and carried him over to the counter, where she doctored his wounds. Then she sat down with him at the kitchen table, and they watched the rose and gold of the February sunset work its magic over the tired, dreary landscape.

"Spring soon," Grace murmured to herself, then glanced at Houdini who had what she could only call a " listening look" on his pointed, almost-human face. "Care for a scritch?" Her fingers ruffled the fur along his neck and shoulders. He butted his head shyly against her hand as the beginnings of a purr starting up inside him. He glanced down at the gray cat, who was lying by the side of the chair, one paw resting on Grace's shoe. The other cat glanced up at Houdini through slitted eyes and returned the purr.

The Siamese tucked his head into the crook of the artist's arm and stretched his right front paw over her wrist. For the first time in weeks, he felt safe.

VII

After a relatively short amount of time, Houdini settled into the household's rhythm. In many ways, it was an easier, more comfortable kind of life than any he'd ever known before. No more sleeping out in a cold tool shed on a winter's night... no more huddling by the dryer vent on a windy day.... And raindrops, he discovered, were kinda fun to watch and bop with your paw when you were on the warm side of the window.

The loss of his left front paw puzzled him greatly. He knew that it had something to do with the road and that big wheel bearing down on him and hurting him so much, he'd ended up in that cage at the clinic; but he couldn't understand what the car or the human driving it would've wanted with his leg. Sometimes, too, he'd imagine that there was feeling still there, even though he could see nothing but a stump.

Slowly, tenaciously, he taught himself to get about on three legs. Walking wasn't so very difficult, but the stairs took some maneuvering. For a long time, he got winded before he was even half-way up or down them. And jumping was just plain beyond him at first. He'd try to leap up onto the narrow edge of the steps, just outside the banister, only to land head-first in the wastebasket alongside the foot of the staircase. Or his legs would splay out from under him, leaving him as helpless as a two-week-old kitten. So he learned to stand up on his hind legs prairie-dog-style and gauge the distance from the floor to the step (or to the top of a bureau or a table or whatever) before making his leaps.

The gray tabby, Merlin, became his friend. They ran races together, Houdini loping gamely after the darker cat, who moved as quickly and as quietly as a shadow. Gradually, the Flame point grew stronger, and they began chasing each other up and down the stairs, making the most unholy racket, their paws sounding like horses' hooves against the wood. And in the afternoons, they curled up together on the blue-and-rust-colored spool quilt on Grace's double bed, their paws wrapped around each other like litter-mates.

Lilah was another story. She'd been abandoned by her first owners, just as Merlin and Houdini himself had been, but at an older age. She'd never gotten over it or the terrible, frightening time she'd been on her own, scavenging for food in a nearby field before the artist had found her. She loved Grace in her own funny way, trailing her devotedly, trilling, and talking to her in a sweet burbly cat-voice that she used for no one else. But something in her held back from trusting anybody, human or feline, completely. She also regarded herself as queen of the household and swatted the two males whenever they got in her way at mealtime or at any other time.

So Houdini learned to keep a respectful distance and to keep his paws off the crocheted toy mice that she hoarded under the coffee table. In return, the black Persian eased up her attacks on him. She never joined in his races or wrestling matches with Merlin; but she took to perching her large, fluffy self on absurdly narrow places—the slender curving arm of the low cricket chair by the little brick fireplace, for instance—where she could watch their antics and their scuffling, purring rustily at them.

Grace, of course, was easy for him to get a fix on. She was so much a cat person that Houdini sometimes thought she was more cat than person; and he soon grew fond of her. He even looked up occasionally when she called him by that silly name she'd given him—Boris—once he realized that she was looking straight at him whenever she said it.

Every morning, he followed the artist up to her workroom, jumped up on the long table there—it was really an old school desk, big enough to seat two people at, its legs spray-painted an electric-blue—and batted her drawing pencils and pastels around while she sketched out designs for her animal sculptures. Those sculptures fascinated Houdini: they were small like cat toys, and he couldn't resist poking at them. They skidded nicely off the table and onto the large braided rug, too. Sometimes, of course, their heads or legs or tails would snap off; then Grace would prim up her mouth and, shaking her head, go fetch the whisk broom and dustpan. The whisk broom was another fascinating toy in Houdini's opinion, but he knew enough not to start any crazy kitten-chasing-its-tail games with her when she was making those quick, angry movements. So he'd lie quietly on the table, peering down at her with that curious, thoughtful look of his; feeling his eyes on her, she'd glance up and smile in spite of herself.

"It's OK, Boris," she'd say gently, reaching up to scritch his ears. "My fault for leaving them within paw's reach." And she'd move some of the sculptures over so that he'd have more room to stretch out. All in all, Houdini was content living with her and her cats. But being content was different from tail-weaving, rolling-in-the-catnip-patch happiness, and somewhere deep inside his cat's soul, he knew it. He enjoyed Merlin's companionship, naturally, but there was part of him that still yearned for Juliet, Dimity, and the kittens. And Cassandra. It was surprising how much the little tigery female had come to mean to him without his knowing it. He felt very much at home with Grace and liked being with her because her ways were, for the most part, quiet and soothing. But he couldn't really love her because he had already given his heart to his girl, and a Siamese only gives his heart to a human once. He never slept on the woman's bed as Merlin and even Lilah did; instead, he'd head down to the cellar at bedtime and curl up in the big wicker laundry basket. There were inevitably some sheets or clothing that Grace hadn't gotten around to folding, and the pleasant lavender smell of the fabric softener she used could sometimes trick him into thinking he was back in Mrs. Leonard's garden, letting the kittens play leap-frog over his wide back....

Every afternoon, Houdini would stand watch at one of the low windows facing the road out in front and wait for the school bus to head up it. He kept waiting for the bus to stop and spit Jill out (for that was what it had seemed to do, back in the days when he and Alexander used to wait for her), but it never did. A few times, when Grace went out to get the afternoon mail, he managed to shoot out the door past her. Each time, he made it as far as the pasture next to her cottage; then, suddenly unsure of his bearings, he'd crouch down and start crying like a kitten separated from its mother. The farmer who owned that particular pasture—a tall, talkative older man who was considered something of an oddity among the other farmers in the community because he always saw to it that his cats were "fixed" and had their distemper shots—would help Grace catch him. Houdini would snuggle down in her arms, grateful for her warmth and caring, but the restlessness inside him remained. And always, always, he was listening for Jill's voice and footstep.

One morning, Grace was sitting in the old gooseneck rocker (Merlin had thoughtfully clawed up the upholstered parts of its arms) in her workroom, sipping her coffee and staring out the window. She was at a complete loss for ideas, and she knew that she needed one more piece—one truly special piece—for the art show that she was getting ready for. Sighing, she turned away from the window (the landscape was really still pretty drab, although her artist's eye could detect some telltale signs of greening) and happened to glance at Houdini lying on the worktable.

The sun was bringing a shimmer to his flame-bright mask and ears, and his eyes ... well, they were as deeply blue as the morning-glories that she planted around the cottage every spring. She made a little trilling noise at him, something she did with all her cats, and he purred back at her, kneading the table's wood with his right front paw. Something clicked in Grace's mind just then. She picked up the drawing pad that had been lying untouched on the floor beside her chair. She sketched slowly, each line and curve giving her pleasure—so closely did the image on the paper resemble what was taking shape in her head. Pausing, the artist looked at the sketch, then at Houdini—or Boris, as she thought of him—and back at the sketch again. She felt that glow that she always did whenever a piece started to come to life for her. She nodded and resumed drawing. By noon, she should be able to finish it, and then tomorrow she could begin roughing out the image in clay.

Grace had always taken great pains with her sculptures, trying to make each one as natural and true to life as possible; but this particular piece seemed to call forth something more from her. She sculpted him in a lying-down position, his remaining front paw tucked under his chest and his long silky tail feathered around him. Only if you looked closely could you see the stump. She wanted people to look at the sculpture and see the cat's ivory-and-red-gold beauty first, not his injury.

She grew even fonder of Houdini as she worked on it, almost as if doing this sculpture made him—well, more hers. Friendly and affectionate as he was, he'd never given his heart into her keeping, not as Merlin had. Of course, Lilah hadn't either, but she'd been sick and badly abused when Grace had taken her in, and the latter had learned to accept what tentative affection the frightened Persian was able to give.

Houdini was different, though. Wherever he'd come from, he didn't act like a cat who'd been mistreated. He liked people—liked Grace, liked her friends, and even liked Dr. Mullen, although the smells and noises of the clinic itself made him jumpy, naturally. Yet there was part of him that held back from Grace, and she sensed it. He was seeking something or someone obviously . . . why else the frequent escapes? And there was a definite pattern to the escapes: they usually took place, oh, say, about 3:30 in the afternoon, and he always headed off in the same direction, toward Mr. Whitcomb's pasture. . . .

But, as her work on the sculpture progressed, the Flame point seemed happier and more at peace in her company. *Maybe*, thought Grace one morning—she was laughingly trying to coax an affectionate but determined Houdini from her chair and he was batting her hand playfully away, defending his territory—*just maybe he's stopped his searching*. And she began to allow herself a flicker of hope.

A few afternoons later, she was just starting to paint in the stripes on the sculpted piece's mask and tail when she heard the Siamese mer-rowing low and pitifully, like she'd never heard him do before. She sat there very still, the brush in her hand dripping its red-gold mixture onto the scarred wooden surface; then she put the brush into the glass of water and turned slowly in his direction.

Houdini was standing atop the low bookcase, his ears and tail quivering. He jumped down onto the braided rug and loped over to the gooseneck rocker by the window facing the road. He hopped up onto the seat—surprisingly graceful, considering both his size and his disability—and from there to the top of the chair. He sat there, his blue eyes watchful and yearning.

Grace eased herself out of her chair, making as little noise as possible. She soon realized, however, that it wouldn't have mattered if she'd slammed the ladder-back chair into her worktable—to Houdini, she had completely ceased to exist. She walked over to the rocker and peered out the window. All she saw was the 3:30 school bus heading up the road past her house. The cat never took those human-ish eyes of his away from it. As it vanished up the hill, his tail drooped, and he shrank into himself.

Grace reached out a hesitant hand, then stroked the back of his head. He turned to her, his blue eyes so wistful, it hurt her to look into them.

The artist stared out the window at the slowly changing landscape. February was spent, the ground wasn't quite as mucky, and the pussywillow below was covered with a slew of velvety gray catkins. But what she was really seeing was Houdini's woebegone face all those times she'd found him crouched in Whitcomb's pasture, calling out as if his life had depended on it. . . . Each time, she'd figured, he'd been crying from fear or cold. Or maybe because, like so many Siamese, he didn't like finding himself left alone too long. Well, he'd been lonely all right, but not for her, fond of her as he was.

Her long slightly curved fingers lingered on his shiny fur. She'd never asked around to see if anyone in the area had lost so unusual a cat, despite what she'd said to Dr. Mullen; she'd simply assumed that he was a stray, another one of the unwanted, just as Merlin and Lilah had been. And then— well, if she had not become all that much a part of his life, he had become so much a part of hers, she couldn't imagine the cottage without him now....

She shook her head and went downstairs to call an ad into the local paper. Houdini, still moping on top of the gooseneck rocker, didn't even notice her going.

One blustery afternoon, about a week later (March was definitely in one of its lion moods that day), Houdini was resting in front of the woodstove with Merlin, as close to it as he could get without singeing his fur. Lilah was curled up in her basket under the antique china cabinet, far enough away from them to suit her psyche but not so far away that she missed out on any of the heat.

The Siamese stretched his front paw out and examined it critically. Could definitely do with a wash, he decided, and began scrubbing it vigorously. Of course, that led to an all-over wash; then, once he'd finished with his own grooming, he started on Merlin, who blinked up at him with sleepy affection. Within seconds, the gray tabby was fully awake, and what had started out as friendly grooming session had turned into an out-and-out tail-biting tussle.

Grace came wandering downstairs with her mug of half-warm tea. She stood listlessly by the foot of the stairs, sipping the brew without even really tasting it. Houdini, having bested his pal in the mock battle, felt her eyes on him and glanced up, his own eyes questioning. She looked, he thought, like she wanted to pat him; but, for some reason, she didn't.

Curious, he remarked to himself. He purred encouragingly at her and rolled over on his side, turning his white belly toward her. She didn't budge. A tad miffed—*What a waste of a good belly*, he told himself indignantly—he rolled over onto his stomach and touched up his fur. Humans. Really.

A car pulled into the driveway. An old car from the sound of it, its growl more of a wheezing and a sputtering. Merlin took off up the stairs—he was a friendly guy but shy around strange humans—and Lilah growled, as she always did whenever she heard an unfamiliar car pull into the yard. But Houdini's ears pricked up. He bolted upright, his tail quivering and his heart doing some pretty amazing twists and turns. There was a knock at the kitchen door, and Grace set the mug down on the circular table-tray of an old floor lamp. Her hand shook like an old woman's, and some of the tea slopped over onto the table-tray, but she never even noticed. She gave Houdini one more long, yearning look, then walked slowly into the kitchen.

The Siamese listened for all he was worth. He heard a babble of voices: one of them was soft and young, its sweetness piercing through him, bringing a rush of memories with it. He was just jumping up to follow it when the artist came back in and lifted him up. She held him close and tight for a moment, her cheek against his fur. Houdini felt her sadness and did his best to lie still—after all, he was fond of her, and he owed her that much for saving him, he knew—although inside, he was squirming with excitement.

Grace carried him into the kitchen and let him slide out of her arms and onto the table. There, right across from him, was his girl, whose voice he'd been listening for all this time. Houdini made his way over to her side of the table and stood up on his hind legs; then he put his lone front paw up on Jill's shoulder and just gazed up at her, all of his cat heart and soul in his eyes. She swallowed hard and gathered him up in her arms. He nestled against her throat, mer-rowing away about his Terrible Time in the parking lot and at the dairy farm and about the Car That Had Taken His Paw Away From Him And Did She Think They Could Get It Back...?

Jill glanced up at Grace from over Houdini's head "Thank you," she said in a shy, choked-up voice. She was trying hard not to cry in front of this strange lady, but her eyes gave her away.

Mr. Leonard was watching his daughter's face and smiling. Then he looked at Grace. "You know, Miss Tyne, we'd all but given up on this feller when my girl saw your ad in the paper there. She'd been feeling pretty down in the mouth about his taking off like that, and it was all the harder for her after we lost two of the other cats. Real pretty fluffy one that the wife was awful fond of got hit by a car; then this funny little calico we got from some old friends of mine upped and disappeared. Just about broke Jill's little heart, it all happening at once like that." He reached over to scritch the Siamese's chin. "Hey, Dirty Harry, whatcha been up to, you rascal? Remember me?" Mr. Leonard saw the stump and drew his breath in sharply, his hazel eyes darkened with pity. "Poor varmint."

He gave the cat a gentle pat, then turned to Grace again. "I know you must've spent a lot getting him fixed up and all," he went on in a lower voice, "and I want to pay you for that."

The artist started to shake her head—she'd gotten a good look at the old clunker outside and, guessing the rest, was ready to eat the costs—then stopped herself when she saw the offended pride in the older man's eyes. She motioned him over toward the rickety little writing desk in the corner. It took some rummaging on her part, but she finally found the vet bill in one of the pigeonholes and handed it over to him, knowing that in doing so, she was handing over all claim to Houdini as well.

Mr. Leonard scanned the bill and gave her a shrewd, friendly look. "But what about the food and all that? I know that must've cost you plenty."

Grace shrugged. "It's OK. He's been company. And I used him as the model for some artwork I'm entering into this show."

He smiled, and the warmth of that smile softened the tired lines of his face and even more so the tired expression in those deep-set eyes that didn't miss much of anything. "Well, thank you—for that and for everything else you did. You saved this little feller's life." He took out his checkbook and pen and scrawled out a check, handing it to her with a nod. "Guess we're all squared away now."

"Yeah, I guess so," replied Grace, trying to match his smile.

Jill, who hadn't had a thought for anybody other than Houdini from the second they walked in the door, heard something in the artist's voice that made her look up. Usually, she didn't like hugging or kissing people that much, but.... Shifting Houdini onto her shoulder, she went over to Grace and kissed her on the cheek. "Thank you," she said awkwardly.

Grace leaned over and touched the child's shoulder gently. As she took her hand away, she let her fingers rest for a moment against Houdini's satiny fur. "Good-bye, Boris," she whispered. She nodded to Mr. Leonard standing over by the back door, and he beckoned to Jill.

The artist watched them, her hand against her throat as if to ease the tightness there. Houdini was draped over the girl's shoulder, the one long reddish-gold paw kneading the soft plushy material of her red winter jacket. His eyes were closed, and if cats could purr up a storm—well, he was calling up a regular hurricane.

"Mr. Leonard," Grace said suddenly. The older man turned away from the door and looked her way, his hick graying eyebrows raised. She swallowed hard. "I'd keep Boris—I mean, Houdini—inside if I were you. I don't know if he can climb trees if he has to get away from dogs or anything. And even if he can climb some, I don't think he'd be able to hold on for very long." She swallowed again, trying to keep the sadness she was feeling from swallowing her whole. "He'd be safer indoors."

Jill's father nodded, his hand resting on the doorknob. "Oh, we won't be taking any chances," he assured the artist. He shook his head. "No more great escapes for you, Dirty Harry. We've been keeping all the cats inside since we lost those last two." He glanced over at his daughter cuddling the big Siamese, then back a Grace. "Thanks again, Miss Tyne."

Grace managed a tiny wave and watched them go. She stood there until she heard the old car chug out of the driveway and down the road. Then she shook herself and walked slowly over to the cats' feeding station. She picked up Houdini's bowl and set it down in the sink. Unable to stand the kitchen's emptiness, she headed upstairs to her workroom. It was empty, too, but she and Houdini had spent so many days there together that some of his red-gold-and-ivory presence seemed to linger. In fact, the life-like little sculpture of him was sitting on the worktable right where she'd left it to dry that afternoon when she'd been given—by God? By the Powers That Be? By the Guardian Spirit of All Cats?—that glimpse into his broken heart and placed the ad.

She pulled up a chair by the worktable and picked up the sculpture, tracing each line and curve of it, smiling a faint, flickering smile. She was still sitting there in the shadows when Merlin came trotting in. He paused on the threshold, looking about for his friend. Then he caught sight of Grace and came running up to her, trilling. He leaped up onto her lap. "Mer-row?" he asked, butting his bullet-shaped head up against her face. Her arms closed around him; he lay down and rested his chin and front paws on her left arm, purring for her and easing, in his own gentle way, the ache that Houdini's going had left behind.

Jill held Houdini all the way home, afraid to let go of him. She didn't even fiddle around with the radio like she usually did. "What's the matter?" her dad asked her with a grin. "Arm stuck?"

"Yep," said Jill, grinning back at him. She gave Houdini a hug. "Dad, can I let him sleep in my room tonight?"

Mr. Leonard laughed. "OK. But just for tonight. Tomorrow night, he gets banished to the cellar with the others, or they'll get jealous and start fighting with him. You gotta keep in mind, sweetheart, they might not remember him after all this time."

"Oh, they'll remember him," Jill replied confidently. Houdini purred and squunked his way through the entire trip home. Here he was, back in his old brown car with all its comforting (from a cat's point of view) smells (although the hole in floorboard had been patched), snuggled up against his girl's coat. He flexed his front paw and blinked up at her adoringly. *See? I was right*, his big blue eyes kept saying. *You did come for me.*

Mr. Leonard chuckled as he shut off the car. "I never saw a cat so glad to get home," he said. And Houdini, looking up into the man's smiling hazel eyes as Jill got out of the car with him, saw that he was glad, too.

The rest of the family gave him a welcome that any cat would be pleased by, especially a Siamese: lots of pats (but not too many—after all, he wasn't a dog, thank you) and a tin of sardines that he polished off immediately. Afterwards, he inspected the living room (it had been a long time since he'd been in it, and they might have made some changes, humans were always moving furniture around and doing silly things like that) and set to work deciphering all the smells about him. He definitely caught a whiff of Alexander's scent on top of the high-backed lady's chair next to the brick fireplace. And that scent on the carpeted scratching post (now, that was something new) on the other side of the fieldstone hearth—why, that was the clover-blossom-and-hay aroma that Cassandra's fur had always had, regardless of what season it was. But both scents were different somehow—duller, less wild. Especially Alexander's.

There were no traces of Juliet or Dimity, although they, too, had always come into the house for regular visits, even after they'd taken up semi-permanent residence at the Deweys'. Now that was a puzzler. Houdini nibbled on the hand-made broom that Mrs. Leonard always kept by the fireplace and considered all the evidence. If he had been human, he would have shaken his head.

Jill, who had been lying on her stomach alongside the hearth and watching him all this time, got up and carted Houdini upstairs to her room before he could investigate any further. The room was just as he remembered it: the braided rug felt just as thick and good to his claws, and the little white bobbles on the bedspread dangled just as teasingly. But he was too exhausted to do more than take a clumsy swipe at them with his paw. So he let his girl hoist him up onto the bed. He lay there, his purrs turning fast into tired squunks. He was home now—all the sad, bad, hungry times had melted away like the morning frost. Even Merlin, Lilah, and the woman, whom he had liked, were no longer as clear to him. He put his big satiny head down on his girl's outstretched hand and drifted off, blissful beyond belief.

VIII

When Jill awoke the next morning, the rainbow happiness of the day before was with her still. But she was feeling awfully stiff, and she couldn't imagine what she was doing half off the bed like this. She pulled herself up and turned around right smack into Houdini. Sometime during the night, the big Siamese had crawled up from his spot on the afghan at the foot of the bed, asking for over more than half of it. The cat lifted his head from the pillow now and was looking at her indignantly. *My bed*, his expression said—*My pillow. Got that?*

Laughing, Jill scritched his head and slipped out of bed. Houdini settled back down among the tumbled bedclothes, trying to make himself very small and failing completely. He was sure she would take him out to the tool shed to join the other cats as soon as she'd gotten dressed; so it puzzled him when she simply straightened out the bed as best she could without disturbing him and left. Another mystery, he decided, just like those cat scents he'd come across last night . . . scents that were familiar yet not familiar. They were around him now, his twitching nose told him, all over the bedding and on the painted headboard, which somebody (who smelled suspiciously like Alexander to him) had clearly marked by rubbing his face all over it.

Jill came back in with a dish of dry cat food in one hand and a yellow crockery bowl of water in the other. She placed both down in front of the old dressing-table that she used as a desk. Houdini crawled out of his blanket-cave and leapt down onto the thick moss-green carpet. He wove in and out between her ankles, mer-rowing his hunger and his happiness. He even got up and tried to do his old kittenish food-dance for her; but he was a little wobbly, being out of practice and having only one front paw to hook into the leg of her jeans. "Oh, Houdini," she said, and there was a catch in her voice that had never been there before.

She watched him for a few minutes before she went back to tidying up the bed. Houdini was still chowing down on the kibble when he heard a scratching on the door-frame. It was followed by a long, drawn-out, haunting miaow. He hastily gulped down the piece of kibble he'd been working on and sat up, his eyes bound and agitated as his old enemy-friend, Alexander, bounded in.

The red tabby hissed at him and puffed out his long striped tail till it was one glorious fat pumpkin-tail. Houdini did likewise. Alexander came closer and sniffed him curiously. The Siamese sniffed him back and wrinkled his long nose. Alexander's scent was different, and so, apparently, was his own. And, just as they'd been with Merlin, the battle maneuvers were just for show.

The long-bodied tabby showed his fangs and raised his paw as if to cuff the younger cat but didn't. Instead, he simply growled him away from the food dish and started to help himself to what was left of the kibble. Houdini sat off to the side for a few seconds. Then he strolled right back over to the yellow-and-white food dish and nudged Alexander over, just so the older cat didn't think he could still boss him around. The two old rivals polished off the rest of the food together, the Czar-cat growling softly whenever he thought the other was inching even a fraction closer to his side of the dish.

The meal over, Alexander jumped up onto the bed for a wash and a nap. Houdini gave the yellow-and-white dish a final swipe with his tongue and worked on his coat till it gleamed ivory, the reddish-gold points glowing like newly minted copper in the sunlight. He glanced around. Alexander was stretched out elegantly on the bedspread watching him out of half-closed eyes. The younger cat picked his way quietly and cautiously across the room and slipped past the half-opened door to the hall.

He sat there for a few minutes, staring at the grandfather clock. *Now, that wasn't here before*, he thought, his head going back and forth with the swinging of its pendulum. If he listened carefully, he could make out this funny, patient clicking noise. *It purrs funny*, he decided. *It's not a cat, but maybe it thinks it's one. Silly thing. I wonder why the humans let it stay?* He moseyed on over to the stairs, only to come muzzle-to-muzzle with Cassandra.

Houdini moved closer for a friendly "hello" sniff. She raised a white-gloved paw at him and hissed briefly; but he understood that this was simply one part of the ritual that he had to put up with in his being re-accepted into the household. So he padded after her, ignoring the matter-of-fact hisses or cuffs she gave him whenever she thought he was stepping out of line. He trailed her all the way up to the attic. She ducked under the eaves and hid behind some old metal milk crates filled with encyclopedias. He ferreted her out, so she scampered over to Mrs. Leonard's cedar chest. She jumped up on it, and from there, took a flying-squirrel leap to the top of a tall, white bookcase, then glared down at him, her ears flattened back like a wild She-cat.

Houdini's front leg began to tire him. He lay down at the foot of the bookcase, determined to wait her out.

The sun that had been dappling the pine floorboards vanished, and the late-afternoon shadows began to take over the attic, swallowing up the odd bits of furniture stashed up there. Houdini yawned, stretched himself, and ambled toward the stairs, his interest in the game flickering and fading. At that moment, Cassandra, the flirty little feline that she was, jumped down from the bookcase. "Ulf," she gasped, for in spite of her lightness, she'd always landed heavily on her paws. She scurried over to Houdini and sniffed him thoroughly, especially his stump. *What happened?* she asked, touching it gently with her paw.

Houdini looked wistfully down his long nose. *The car took it.*

Oh. Her green eyes became wary. *The car took Juliet, too. I saw.* Then, before he could find out what she meant, she cuffed him playfully and raced past him down the attic stairs. Houdini sprang after her, forgetting his missing paw and his questions. They were suddenly kittens again, flying like furry little dervishes through the rustling field-grasses and fleabane of memory.

He spent the rest of that afternoon wrestling and playing paw-poke with Cassandra. She showed him all kinds of hiding places: the shadowy under-the-bed places, the narrow cave-like crawlspace at the back of Jill's closet, and the bottom shelf of the linen closet with all those thick clean towels to lie on. But Houdini preferred Jill's little low cricket chair with its moss-green cushions, slightly faded from the room's direct sunlight. He could lie there, safe, snug, and dignified, and keep an eye on everything going on in the big green-and-gold room. *It's all the same,* he marveled, as he went over his front paw one more time (having only one left in front, he felt very protective of it and gave it extra attention), *but it's different, too. I could get used to this. . . .*

When it was time for their late meal of the day, Jill didn't shoo them all out to the tool shed, as he had expected. Instead, she led the three cats down to the cellar. A flower-sprigged loveseat, too shabby for the living room, had been hauled down there and placed across from the dryer and washer. To the right of the loveseat was an old wicker laundry basket, its decorative edging all broken off, that Jill had salvaged from the trash and made a large calico cushion for. Two litter boxes were tucked away in the unused hatchway.

Houdini just stood there, taking it all in. He had never been in the cellar before: it was dampish and smelled of old machinery, oil, and paint (there were two workbenches down there, one covering the length of the wall from the window to Scott's darkroom, the other shorter and wider and situated across from Mr. Leonard's glass-cutter), apples, potatoes (there were bushel baskets of both by the hatchway), and, of course, cats. He thought he could detect something of Sassy's and Peri's scents mingled with Alexander's and Cassandra's—fainter and older, but definitely theirs. But he didn't see them, and this confused him greatly.

Of Juliet and Dimity there was nothing. He had no way of knowing, of course, that Juliet was dead; that Dimity, like Daphne before her, had run off soon afterwards; or that his kittens had recently gone to live with Jodi, the young woman in charge of Jill's 4-H group. To Cassandra and Alexander, the other cats were simply gone, and the how or the why of their going meant little to them. But Houdini, with his Siamese hypersensitivity, felt a terrible wistfulness gnawing upon him like a hunger, especially in regard to his Juliet.

Alexander and Cassandra brushed past him, and he shook off the sadness, coming back with a whoosh to the present. He followed them, scoping out their special feeding places. Alexander's was the top of a badly scarred maple bureau, which Mrs. Leonard stored old photos and what was left of the boys' old train sets in; Cassandra's was one end of a long old-fashioned metal table, painted white, that sat alongside it. At the other end of the table was an odd green metal chair, which had come out of the old milk room at Mr. Leonard's father's farm. Jill looked at Houdini and patted the chair seat. He stood up on his hind legs, judging the distance, then sprang up onto it. From there, it was an easy jump onto the table-top, where a bowl was waiting for him.

Soon the cellar was filled with the sound of the three cats purring and crunching away. It was, Houdini thought, like the old days out in the shed. Almost.

Afterwards, he and Cassandra chased each other around, over, and under around the worn-out unwanted pieces of furniture, leaping out at each other from the shadows. When it grew very dark, Jill came down to play with them for a bit before shutting them in the cellar for the night. Once she was gone, Alexander yawned and lopped up on the loveseat, which was, he told the Siamese with a flash of his teeth (he had only six of them left and nothing to brag about at that, but he knew how to make the most of them), his personal property. Cassandra jumped back up onto the white table for a last wash-and-preening session before bedtime. Houdini investigated the wicker basket, liking the smell of the cedar chips that Jill had stuffed the big cushion with, but not completely satisfied with it.

It needs something, he decided and, out of inspiration, moseyed over to the basket that held all the dirty laundry. Cassandra watched him closely, her little lion-cub's face friendly and curious. Houdini rooted through the laundry till he found one of his girl's socks. He picked it up in his mouth and carried it triumphantly back to the other basket. *That's better,* he thought, settling down on the wine-colored calico cushion and sniffing his find appreciatively. He kneaded the sock, drooling a bit and burbling a purr-song of belonging.

Within a few days, Houdini had settled just as comfortably into the new routine at his old home. He still kept looking for Juliet and the others, though.

One morning, after he'd been back a few weeks, the weather had warmed up enough for Jill to let them all out on the back porch to play. Houdini and Cassandra raced out, as giddy as kittens having their first snort of catnip; Alexander, ever-conscious of his dignity as Senior-Cat-in-Residence, sauntered out, sniffing the April air coming through the slightly open jalousie windows in that casual, almost bored way he perfected.

The porch had been fixed up into a sitting room since Houdini had stayed there as a kitten. Houdini tried his claws out on the teal carpet (*Good stuff,* he thought: *I can really get my claws into this*), and looked around him. Then he spied an African violet sitting on the cobbler's-bench coffee table, flaunting its large purply looms at him. Why, that plant was just asking for it. The big cat jumped up on the table, ready for the kill. An old jacket of Jill's happened to be lying next to the plant in its pretty blue-and-white porcelain pot. Houdini sniffed it, then drew back, snarling: he smelled blood and death in the faded brown cloth and another smell that was warm and she-cattish, as wildly sweet and familiar as the catnip and the other herbs that he and Juliet had once romped through in the garden....

The jacket was the one that Jill had been wearing when she and Timmy Fitzgerald had found Juliet lying rushed and bloody along the roadside; Mrs. Leonard had scrubbed at the bloodstains with every kind of cleaning solution imaginable, but still they lingered, their smell horribly strong to a cat. Houdini did an about-face and jumped down from the table, crying even harder than he had when he'd been searching for Jill out in Mr. Whitcomb's field.

The jacket disappeared soon afterwards. Jill refused to wear it now, and Mrs. Leonard didn't try to make her. She herself couldn't even look at it; she'd been very fond of Juliet despite all the hens and chickens that the fluffy tiger cat used to dig up in her garden. But, for a long time, Houdini refused to go out on the porch.

He understood that there was no point in searching any longer, that the blood-scent was Juliet's and that he would never see her again. He didn't know what had happened to Dimity or the kittens, but he sensed that they, too, were gone from his life for good. The time he'd been away made his sense of loss a little less sharp than it might otherwise have been. Then, too, he had the other cats to keep him company. He and Alexander, their battling tomcat urges gone, more or less declared a ceasefire. And Cassandra became his second self, shadowing him from room to room.

He missed the field, the garden, and all those wonderful climbable maple and pine trees less than might have been expected. They, too, belonged to another life. Besides, before the spring was over, Mr. Leonard had built a cat enclosure out of chicken wire and scrap umber, a regular "Gilligan's Island" contraption, with a let door set in one of the cellar windows that they could easily butt open with their heads. The three cats took to spending most of their days out in the enclosure. There, from behind a screen of ferns and forsythia bushes, they would watch rabbits, birds, and squirrels unobserved, their tails twitching and their eyes aglow.

Once in awhile, a chipmunk would cluelessly wander in (*Are they stupid or what?* Houdini would remark to Cassandra, and she would twitch her whiskers in agreement), and a Great Safari would commence. Alexander, the aggressive Czar-cat that he was, usually ended up making the kill; but once, the Siamese managed to nab the tail off a chipmunk and brought it inside, where he paraded around the kitchen with it till Mrs. Leonard made Jill take it away from him and heave it outside. Houdini was, as he told Jill in a series of long drawn-out miaows—or, in his case, bleats—Very Insulted by This, and he sat around for a long time, staring at her out of reproachful cross-eyes, Not Sure if He Could Forgive Her. A chaw of catnip from the herb garden made him decide to view the matter more charitably, however: the tail hadn't had much meat on it, to begin with, and what would he have done with it after awhile, anyway? A whole chipmunk, on the other hand . . . now, that would've been another story. . . .

Cassandra, whom he generously shared some of the catnip with, agreed with him. *It was pretty stringy,* she told him. She nuzzled what was left of the purply-blue catnip blossoms. *This smells nicer, too.* And then they suddenly went kittenish, rolling about on their backs, their paws flailing happily about in the air.

But the best times, as far as Houdini was concerned, were still the ones when he had Jill all to himself. Making himself small—well, as small as possible (he still thought of himself as a kitten despite his big, stocky build and was always squeezing himself into the smallest boxes and spaces imaginable)—he'd snuggle up in the crook of her arm while she read. And he'd stay like that for hours, only stirring himself now and then to wash between his toes or chew the tassels off Jill's bookmarks. Sometimes, when he was done with all that, he'd wash Jill, too, sandpapering her eyelids or the insides of her ears with his rough pink tongue. Then, pleased with his efforts (human ears were tough-to-clean things, with all those peculiar ridges inside), he'd settle back down to dreams of chasing moles and deer-mice out in the old garden or running races with a long-haired tiger cat in fields turned pinkish-gold by the sunset.

IX

"Are you sure you want to take Houdini to the pet show this year?" Mrs. Leonard asked hesitantly over breakfast one Saturday morning in late May. She and her husband exchanged glances. "He's been through a lot this year, honey. Maybe Cassandra would be the better one for you to take. Or Solstice. They're both beautiful little cats."

Solstice was a four-month-old Ruddy Abyssinian kitten that the antiques dealer down the road had given Jill. The dealer, Mrs. Hape, bred Abys on the side, and sometimes, now that she was older, Jill looked in on the stay-at-home cats for her when she was away at a show. The little amber-eyed quick-pawed Aby was, Mrs. Hape explained to the Leonards, her way of showing how much she appreciated all the help that Jill had been giving her around the cattery.

"Maybe some day she'll be a breeder, too," Mrs. Hape had remarked. "She really has a way with the cats. I mean, she's a natural." Mr. Leonard had groaned.

The "natural" put down the bagel she'd been buttering and glared at her parents now. Adults could be so—she scrambled about in her head for a word, then fell back on a favorite one of Mrs. Hape's—*pig-headed,* she told herself, ignoring her own particular pig-headedness just then. "I can take Solstice next year," she said grabbing the kitten and stopping her from a frontal assault on the lonely, unguarded bagel. "And Cassandra's too skittish. You know how she hides on top of the cupboards in the cellar whenever people come over. She'd hate going."

Again, there was that wordless exchange between her parents. Mr. Leonard cleared his throat. "Sweetheart," he said gently, "we know Houdini means the world and more to you. But he's missing that leg, and I don't think the judges are gonna see much beyond that. You'd come home without any kind of ribbon at all and feeling pretty down in the mouth for all your trouble."

"He would win a ribbon," Jill insisted, not taking her dark eyes away from her father's face. "He's still beautiful. And none of the other kids'll have a Flame point Siamese either."

"Now, you don't know for sure he's a purebred, like this little one here—," Mr. Leonard began.

"Well, he looks just like that picture of one that I saw in Mrs. Hape's cat magazine," she argued, "and I'm taking him." She took a bite out of her bagel and chewed defiantly. Of course, Solstice would be the logical choice. Jill had no doubt that the playful little Abyssinian with her rich ticked tarnished-copper coloring, apricot underbelly, and whiskers that looked so comically big against her tiny face would win some sort of ribbon. But Houdini was beautiful, too. Both Mrs. Hape and Miss Tyne had said so, and one being a breeder and the other an artist, they would know best, wouldn't they? "Miss Tyne's sculpture of him won a prize at that exhibition," Jill blurted, clutching at the memory of the photo and clipping that Grace had recently sent her.

Her father shook his head kindly. "That was something she just made up to look like old Dirty Harry here. And it didn't really show where he was missing that leg of his. Now, you know, I think the world of this white rascal, too"—Mr.

Leonard bent over to ease Houdini away from the plastic tub of cream cheese that he was trying to hook with his right paw while standing up on his hind legs—"but you gotta remember, other people are gonna look at him and see only that stump of his and nothing else."

"I'm taking him," Jill repeated. She offered the rest of her bagel to Houdini, who promptly licked all the butter off it and left it for Solstice to play hockey around the kitchen with. He then strolled over to the curio shelf that Mr. Leonard had built out of old mirror and jalousie window glass for his wife. The mirrored back came almost all the way down to the floor. The Siamese sat down and preened himself in it until his coat shimmered in the sunlight. He glanced up at Jill and winked at her. "Mer-row," he said happily, and began purring loudly, just as if she had touched him. *He'll win something, I know he will*, she told herself, and crossed her fingers under the table.

So, that next Saturday, Houdini found himself riding in state to the school pet show. Jill had bathed him the night before despite his most heart-rending bleats; she had also saved up her allowance and bought him a purple velveteen collar splattered with rhinestones. He peered out of the grid-like door of the cat carrier that Mrs. Hape had lent Jill and nuzzled his girl's fingers. It was, he decided, a very different way of riding from what he was used to but much more comfortable, what with this faded, old flannel baby blanket under him and all. He yawned and poked his paw out one of the grids as far as he could. *You haven't patted me in the last five minutes*, he telegraphed at Jill with his eyes, but she was all keyed up about the show and didn't notice.

The pet show was being held on the field out by the playground at Jill's school. Her dad left her off at the main entrance to the old redstone building and told her he'd be back at one o'clock, after the judging was over. Jill, her mind only half on what he was saying, nodded and headed across the playground with its makeshift little face-painting and game booths all decked out in purple, gold, and red crepe paper. She picked out a pretty shady spot by some poplar and white birch trees near the edge of the field, right next to Doreen, a pleasant brown-haired girl from her 4-H troop who'd brought her miniature rabbit, Blackberry. The shade would make it easier for Houdini to get through the show, and there'd be room for Kathy, too, when she showed up with her new black half-Persian kitten, Bandit.

Jill took Houdini out of the carrier and clipped an old dog leash to his fancy new collar. (Last year, when she'd brought Alexander, he'd been so put off by all the people and their noise, he'd tried to leg it out to the street.) The Siamese took it all in his stride. He rubbed his head against her hand and began nibbling at the grass. He was intrigued by the noises and the animal smells all right, but not particularly worried. After his Great Adventure, an elementary-school pet show was really pretty tame, and besides, he had his girl there with him. He sniffed Doreen and found her acceptable (although he was, of course, much more interested in getting up close and personal with Blackberry), and he liked Timmy Fitzgerald, who came strolling up just then with his dog, Penrod. Usually, Houdini didn't have much use for dogs, but Penrod was a collie-corgi mix and about "half-a-dog high and two-dogs long," as Timmy said. Not too threatening. Besides, Houdini knew that Penrod was terrified of cats, thanks to the Fitzgeralds' cat, Toto, who'd scratched him on his collie-long snout back in his puppy days.

So, how's it going? Houdini sauntered up to the little brown dog, who backed up onto Timmy's foot.

Fine—just fine, Penrod responded in a half-whimper.

Houdini sat down and made a big show of examining his front claws. This was fun. *No cracks about the leash, got it?*

Got it, said Penrod. He was definitely beyond the half-whimper stage at this point.

Doreen was talking about the 4-H fair—it wasn't till the end of the summer, but she'd already made up her mind that with her mom's help, she was going to try to make a tiny lap quilt for it and enter Blackberry in that, too, of course—and Timmy was telling them both a long, exaggeratedly funny story about the last Boy Scouts camp-out he'd been on when a jeering sing-song voice broke through their good time.

"Look who brought her kitty!" it hooted.

Jill didn't even bother glancing around. She knew that voice all too well. Kelly Benson sat behind her in math. she had long blonde hair and a weasel-face and had managed all by herself to add a whole new dimension to Jill's hatred of that particular subject.

With Kelly was Margie Hall, who wasn't exactly a mean girl but wasn't much of anything else. She basically just acted as Kelly's echo. Jill ignored them both. It was the only way she'd found of dealing with Kelly, and Margie—well, Margie was such a stick figure of a person, it was easy to forget she was there at all.

Kelly's hard little blue eyes flickered over Houdini, who was checking out a large red-clover blossom. He was very fond of clover and often ate the four-leafed ones that Jill brought in from the yard before she could stop him.

"Is that the best you could do, Leonard?" she asked, staring hard at the stump where the Siamese's left paw had been. Jill winced. Kelly saw the wince and went in for the kill, her eyes glittering. "That cat's as ugly as you are, with just that big bumpy thing there instead of leg. Gross! Makes me wanna puke! You must be a real dip if you think the judges'll give you a prize for that."

"No, I expect that the dip prize would definitely be yours," Timmy shot back on his friend's behalf.

Jill appreciated his defending her—when it came to sarcasm, Timmy was already the undisputed champion of the fifth grade—but she knew it was time for her to stand up for herself. "I'd rather be what I am than what you are!" she flashed, gathering the cat up in her arm. Houdini, sensing her distress, nuzzled her face sympathetically. *She sounds like a blue jay. Can I bite her?*

"Yeah, bet you both crawled out from under a rock!" the other girl shrilled. "I despise you! The whole school—"

"Hello, Jill." Dr. Mullen's friendly, slightly gravelly voice cut through Kelly's ranting like a scalpel. "This Houdini cat of yours is looking mighty handsome and glossy today. I don't believe that the judges'll have seen a Flame point Siamese before, certainly not one with a fine, thrifty build like his. So many Siamese are terribly inbred. But this fellow's a beauty."

Jill turned to the vet with a smile. Grace Tyne had given the Leonards Dr. Mullen's name, and they'd begun taking the cats to him on a regular basis. He always explained to Jill exactly what he was doing, talking to her in the same blunt, matter-of-fact way that he did to adults.

Kelly mumbled something under her breath and slunk away, Margie trailing after her. Jill put Houdini back on the grass, and Timmy knelt down to pat him. "He's a good 'un," the boy said appreciatively. Then, putting on his most deadpan face, he looked up and said, "Say, Jill, I got an old T.V. table leg I saved at home—y'know, one of the ones with a wheel on the end?" He traced out a rough shape in the air with his hands. "I could put a kinda sling on the end for Houdini's stump, and he could get around even better than he does now—shoot, he could skate in the Winter Olympics."

Dr. Mullen chuckled. "Keep working on that one Timmy—keep working." He let his gaze stray over to the face-painting booth, where Kelly and Margie were hanging out now. "Never liked that girl." He shook his head. "She had this little black-and-white kitten that she used to bring in to me whenever she and her parents thought about it, which wasn't often. I don't know that she actually mistreated the little scrapper, but she certainly neglected it. Worst mats I ever saw and an abscess so bad, the side blew out. I lambasted them unmercifully for that one, I tell you. Kitten finally took off, and I don't know of too many cats that'll do that unless they're dying."

"And they never found it?" Jill asked, remembering Daphne and Dimity—and, of course Houdini's own disappearance—and interested in spite of herself.

Dr. Mullen took off his horn-rims and rummaged trough his sports-jacket pocket for a big, white work handkerchief. He began buffing the lenses and humming a little to himself. When he looked up, his blue-gray eyes were smiling. "Well, it is curious," he said slowly, "but my granddaughter has this handsome black-and-white cat now. Calls it 'Woody'— that's short for 'Woodruff X. Stray,' says she. Of course, my son's place is miles away from where the Bensons live, so it wouldn't seem likely it's the same cat." He put his glasses back on and gave Jill a sharp glance. "Point is, that cat knew he didn't have to put up with that kind of treatment. And neither do you."

Jill fixed her eyes on Houdini, who was padding through the grass, intent on a grasshopper; and Timmy and Doreen had the grace to step back a ways and busy themselves with their own pets. After a few moments, the older vet began speaking again, his voice more casual. "I always enjoy these pet shows," he remarked. "Of course, I haven't been able to make it the last few years. Got a cat bite a couple of years ago that sent me into the hospital with a nasty infection. Thought I was going to die. Lost twenty pounds. I needed to, but that's beside the point. Then, last year, my heart was acting up, and I had to make this little trip I hadn't planned on back there."

"Dr, Mullen," Jill blurted out, "do you think I was wrong to bring Houdini here?"

"Wrong?" The gray-haired man looked at her curiously. "Never occurred to me that right and wrong had anything to do with it." He pushed his glasses back up his nose and smiled. "No, Jill, I don't. Oh, I expect some folks might call it 'foolish,' but I make a point of going with my gut and not listening overmuch to that kind of thing. Houdini's a very handsome specimen of cat and one who's made it against some very tough odds, to boot. He may not get a prize, but he certainly deserves one." Dr. Mullen sighed. "People are funny about illness and disabilities like Houdini's. They have trouble dealing with anything less than perfection, though where they find that, I haven't the faintest. They don't seem to be able to get it through their thick human skulls that a person or an animal can have a good life despite disabilities and what-not."

He stared for what felt like a long time across the road at some peach trees that were deep coral-pink with blossom; when he spoke again, his voice was—well, different somehow, Jill thought. Less brisk and matter-of-fact. Almost as if he was talking to himself, she decided. "You know, Jill, some people might consider my heart disease a disability. In fact, a lot of my clients are forever asking me why I don't retire and just tend to my horses. Well, I can't do that. I love my work, and giving it up would be giving up a very big part of myself.

"I'm not going to settle for less than a full life," he continued. "Why should Houdini? If I had honestly believed that he would be leading less than a full life with three legs, I would have advised Grace Tyne to let me put him down the day that she brought him in to me." Dr. Mullen patted Jill on the shoulder. "I've got to be getting on home now. One of my mares is due to foal any minute now, and I'm feeling a tad anxious about her. Good luck to you both. I'll say 'hi' to Miss Tyne for you when she brings Merlin and Lilah in for their shots next week." He scritched Houdini's head. "Give 'em hell, Harry."

Jill watched the stocky figure stroll across the field, stopping to chat briefly with the some of the other kids and their parents or take a better look at whatever animal had snagged his eye. Then she turned back to Houdini, who had been stalking a bird—in his mind, at least—and who was rubbing up against her ankles now. "Mer-row?" he asked.

She picked him up again—more for her sake than for his—and rested her cheek against his satiny white fur. *We're going to do it, Houdini,* she told him silently. *We'll show them.*

"Wah-wuh," the Siamese replied. He sensed that she was on edge, although not as much as she had been when the blue jay girl had been bothering her. He butted his face against hers and gave her a cat-food-flavored kiss right smack on the lips.

Doreen and Timmy moseyed back over; and pretty soon, Kathy joined them with Bandit. The kitten was a big hit with his plushy black coat and enormous golden eyes— "He looks like an inkblot!" squealed Doreen—and Houdini, who was as paternal as he was wide, gave him a paw's up as well. He showed the little guy a particularly nice patch of clover and gave him a rundown on the things he needed to know. Well, at least, for the duration of the show. *The dog*—he glanced scathingly in Penrod's direction—*is afraid of us. Remember that.*

Yes, sir, replied Bandit, anxious to make a good impression on the big cat.

Jill and Kathy fell to talking about the clubhouse they were building in the Deweys' large garden—they built a new one every spring, always in a different place—and both Timmy and Doreen had some good suggestions to make. So it only seemed fair to invite them to join in on it, too. Kathy also wanted to explore the new houses that were being built below the Leonards' field and check out some tracks she thought belonged to deer-jackers. She'd heard shots coming from the woods the last few nights, she claimed. Timmy wasn't sure he bought the deer-jacker story but said he'd probably go along just in case. Doreen, who'd gotten a little pale at the part about the guns, said she'd pass.

"Yeah, out," teased Timmy. The brown-haired girl reddened, then laughed and admitted he was probably right.

"Hey, Jill. Written any more stories?"

That was Mr. Logan, her science and creative writing teacher. Jill didn't do well in science—she just couldn't seem to keep the details straight, no matter how often she read over the chapters or how many different ways Timmy came up with to explain things to her—but she loved writing stories. She was very big on ghost stories and the Narnia books just then, so her own tales were filled with vampires, ghosts, unicorns, talking badgers and lions, and, of course, the occasional magic-working cat. Mr. Logan gave her Ds on most of her science tests and quizzes; but he always enjoyed her stories and read them aloud to the class whenever he could. Jill shrugged off the Ds; the stories were, after all, what mattered.

She was just starting to tell Mr. Logan about the story she was working on now when she saw the ribbon. Big and purple-and-gold and gaudy as all get-out, attached to the teacher's shirt pocket. There was a shorter fussy-looking man standing behind him whom Jill recognized him as Mr. O'Dell, one of the sixth-grade math teachers. He, too, wore a rosette. She gulped back the rest of her words.

Somehow, knowing that Mr. Logan was one of the judges made Jill feel—well, not so much at home with him as she usually did. She wondered if he would see Houdini as Dr. Mullen, Mrs. Hape, and Miss Tyne did, with eyes that knew how to see beyond the outward shape of things, or if he'd only see the stump, just as Dad had predicted. So many of the other kids had brought big-eyed calendar kittens like Bandit, all sailboat ears and velvety paws. A sixth-grade girl, whom Jill knew by sight, had brought a smoke-gray Persian with glowing copper eyes. There was even one flirty Seal point Siamese who kept grabbing playfully at any passers-by who drifted close enough to her cage.

Houdini, his blue eyes were quick to catch the slightest movement, stood up on his hind legs and made lightning grabs for the ball-point pen that Mr. Logan was twirling around between his fingers. "Hello," the science teacher laughed, reaching down to pat Houdini's head. The Flame point had managed to get his claws snagged on the teacher's shirt cuff. Handing the clipboard and brown envelope in his other hand over to Jill, Mr. Logan squunched down and carefully eased the claws out of the fabric. "Who's this fellow, Jill? He's not the one from your stories, is he?"

"No, that's Alexander. This is Houdini," explained the girl, her voice low and hesitant. Then she went on to tell him Houdini's story—about David's finding him in the empty on-campus apartment, about their smuggling him onto the airplane, and about his disappearance and everything he'd gone through. Or, at least, as much as Miss Tyne and Dr. Mullen had been able to tell her. She spoke truly and from the heart, forgetting her nervousness. Her teacher listened quietly, never taking his thoughtful dark eyes from the cat. She almost told him about Miss Tyne's sculpture and the prize it had won the exhibit but stopped herself. If Mr. Logan and Mr. O'Dell awarded Houdini a ribbon, it had to be because of Houdini himself, not because of that.

"Well, he's had quite a time of it," Mr. Logan remarked. He stood up and nodded to his companion "Mr. O'Dell and I are going to have to make some track if we're to get the judging done by noon, but we'll be back." He smiled at her, and then he and Mr. O'Dell were over to take a look at Bandit and Blackberry before moving onto the next row of animals. Timmy, who had just come along to the show to see how Houdini would make out—"for moral support," as Mr. Leonard was wont to say—ambled over with Penrod. "I think they liked your story," he said quietly. "You could see them listening, if you know what I mean." He patted Houdini. "Told you he was a good 'un."

"Yeah, you did," she agreed, gladder than ever that he was her friend.

More waiting. She tried to keep her mind on her friends' conversation. Kathy had some ideas for the new moss garden they were starting to build in the Leonards' side yard (they liked to spread their projects over the two yards). Timmy, who was a born junk collector, had just come up with a new scheme he called his "Something-for-Nothing" deal: people gave him their old T.V. sets, broken radios, and such, and he took them away for free. He thought it was a pretty cool deal, but his mom didn't, he said. Jill listened and laughed, but her thoughts kept dancing all over the place like restless spirits.

Houdini, deciding that it was time for a lap, climbed up onto hers. He curled up in the crook of her left arm, stretched his paw over her wrist, and rested his head on it. Jill tightened her other arm around his back-end to keep him from spilling off her lap, he was so big. Not fat, just so big and muscular, it was hard to believe that he'd practically fit in the palm of her hand when David had brought him to her.

Leaning over, she gave him a gentle squeeze. She wanted this ribbon for him so badly. Oh, she knew the prizes were for really silly things—last year, Alexander had won a blue ribbon for "the longest tail," and Kathy's old cat, Elsa, had taken a red for "the most beautiful eyes," but it still mattered to her all the same. Maybe because Houdini mattered so much to her. She had never had a cat quite like him. But it was more than that. She had lost him, and he had come back to her and so was doubly precious to her.

Jill was still resting her cheek against Houdini's fur when Timmy nudged her and pointed to the judges heading back their way. They stopped in front of Kathy first and handed her a blue ribbon for Bandit. "For the prettiest eyes," Mr. Logan said and grinned. "Guess you know how to pick 'em, Kathy."

Blackberry got a blue ribbon, too, "for the plushiest coat." Then the teachers came to Jill, and Mr. Logan looked at Jill—then at Houdini resting complacently on her lap, the lone front paw draped possessively over her arm—and then back at Jill again.

He cleared his throat. "Jill," he said gently, "we didn't know what to do about this fellow of yours. You see, we've never had a handicapped pet brought to the show before, and none of the usual categories seemed to fit."

Uh-oh, thought Jill, this is it. *So Mom and Dad—and Kelly—were right, and Dr. Mullen and my other friends were wrong.* The day all at once lost its blue-and-gold shimmer. She tried to come up with a smile for her teacher, but she could feel her lips quivering and knew that it wasn't a very good one.

"That doesn't mean that Houdini here doesn't deserve something," Mr. Logan continued, handing his judge's paraphernalia over to Mr. O'Dell. He unpinned the ribbon from his shirt and fastened it to the back of Houdini's collar, where it streamed out behind him in all its sunset glory of colors. Then he straightened himself back up and smiled at Jill.

Jill glowed. Suddenly, the day became beautiful blue-and-gold again, just like her grandmother's lusterware tea set in the corner cabinet back home. Like Houdini's eyes and markings. It didn't matter that the ribbon's colors were slightly faded now or that Mr. Logan must've absent-mindedly rubbed his ink-stained fingers against it at some point during the judging; to Jill, it was more beautiful than all her 4-H ribbons put together, and she was pretty proud of those. But some day, when she had tossed those in the trash, she knew that she would still have this one, tucked away with Alexander's blue one and the poem that Timmy had clipped out of the newspaper for her in her special sky-blue jewelry box with the white cats on it.

She couldn't hug her teacher, so she lifted Houdini off her lap and hugged him instead. She hadn't felt like this since Mr. Logan had read one of her poems aloud in creative-writing class and one of the kids had clapped and whistled, shouting out, "That's a Jill Leonard special!" She peered over Houdini's fur at the two men and smiled shyly. Mr. O'Dell reached out an uncertain hand toward the cat. Houdini sniffed the stubby fingers—they smell friendly, he decided—and rubbed his head sociably against them.

"Well, how about that now?" exclaimed Mr. O'Dell. He shook his head. "My mother-in-law's cat is a Siamese, too, and real snooty. But this fella's something—almost as good as a dog."

Houdini looked up, sensing that he was being talked about. Then, noticing that Mr. O'Dell's ribbon was a tad frayed around the edges, he decided to help it along some. He grabbed at it—and Jill grabbed at him—but the Siamese definitely had the upper paw and wasn't going to relinquish his newfound toy without a fight. The fact that it was attached to a strange human didn't faze him in the least.

It took some doing (and a bit of skin, as Houdini was in the mood for a little paw-boxing), but Jill final managed to pull him off the ribbon. "I'm sorry, Mr. O'Dell," she gasped, setting the Siamese down on the grass.

But the short man only chuckled rustily. He unpinned his judge's ribbon and tossed it down for the big cat. "Here you go, fella," he said. "Go for it."

And that, in Houdini's eyes, was undoubtedly the best ribbon of the day.

Cassandra was waiting for him in Jill's room when they got back from the pet show. She looked up from the green-yellow-and-white afghan on the bed where she'd been napping and yawned, giving her friend an affectionate nuzzle. He returned the nuzzle enthusiastically, and they bathed each other for an ecstatic purr-filled half-hour or so, Houdini telling her about the pet show in his chatty Siamese fashion. Afterwards, they played with the ribbons that Jill had left on her desk, knocking them onto the floor and kicking and biting all the freshness out of them.

Cassandra tired of the game before he did and headed downstairs to the enclosure. Houdini half-heartedly pawed at a ribbon; but without his playmate to join in the pretending, it had become just a boring piece of silk and not a wonderfully slithery creature that he could pounce on and shake about in his mouth. He hopped up onto the desk and into the open window, arranging himself comfortably against the screen. His tail witched slightly, and he made some low chattering noises at the birds who were outside by the feeder, pecking about for seed in the thick, cool grass where he'd once played with Juliet and Dimity.

He watched a young rabbit nibble at the red clover rowing by the stone lamp post before a rustling noise from underneath the spruce hedge sent it bolting for cover. The new neighbor's cat—a gray-striped half-Manx with a round little body and a kitten's face, his stub of a tail sticking up like a broken pitcher handle, went dashing after it.

A big silvery-gray raccoon came loping into the yard. Houdini had caught glimpses of him from the windows from time to time: he mostly hung out in the backyard, not far from the old tool shed, but sometimes he wandered into the front to pull down the birdfeeder with his clever paws. He, too, had lost a leg—his right hind one—in a trap and, during his convalescence, had gotten into the habit of foraging during the day. Only once, the Siamese noted, when a car came rumbling up the driveway and startled him, did the raccoon turn just a tad too quickly and almost tumble over himself.

Houdini yawned. Jill had left her red sweater lying on the desk, right next to the dainty white lamp with ivy painted on the shade. Houdini nuzzled the wool happy at the safe, familiar smell of his girl. He pushed and pulled at the sweater with his front paw, making a nest out of it for himself. In the golden-glow of the late afternoon, he looked very much like Grace Tyne's sculpture of him. He lay there, his eyes half-closed and his purr burbling over, sweeter than birdsong.

About the Author

T.J. Banks is the author of *Souleiado* and *Catsong*. Her work has appeared in numerous journals and anthologies, including *Soul Menders, Their Mysterious Ways, The Simple Touch of Fate, A Cup of Comfort for Women in Love, Chicken Soup for the Single Parent's Soul,* and Guideposts' *Comfort from Beyond* series. A Contributing Editor to *laJoie* and former stringer for the Associated Press, she has received awards for her work from the Cat Writers' Association (CWA), ByLine, and The Writing Self. She lives with her daughter, Marissa, and their cats and rabbits in a sometimes peaceable but always interesting kingdom in Connecticut.